Edited by
Jeannette L. Faurot

New York London
Toronto Sydney
Tokyo Singapore

Asian-Pacific Folktales and Legends

A Touchstone Book
Published by Simon & Schuster

TOUCHSTONE
Rockefeller Center
1230 Avenue of the Americas
New York, NY 10020

TOUCHSTONE and colophon are registered trademarks of Simon & Schuster Inc.

Designed by Elina D. Nudelman
Manufactured in the United States of America

10 9 8 7 6 5 4 3 2 1

Library of Congress Cataloging-in-Publication Data

Asian-Pacific folktales and legends/edited by Jeannette Faurot.
    p.   cm.
    "A Touchstone Book."
    1. Tales—East Asia. 2. Tales—Asia, Southeastern. 3. Legends—East Asia. 4. Legends—Asia, Southeastern. I. Faurot, Jeannette.
GR330.A75   1995   95-31549
398.2´095—dc20   CIP

ISBN 0-684-81507-9 (hardcover)
ISBN 0-684-81197-9 (paperback)

PERMISSIONS:

ASIAN FOLKLORE STUDIES
"Three Fox Stories," from "The Acolyte and the Fox," "The Old One-eyed Man," and "The Fox at Hijiyama," translated by Fanny Hagin Mayer, in *Folklore Studies*, Vol. XI.1, Peking, 1952. [*Folklore Studies* is the predecessor to *Asian Folklore Studies*.] Reprinted by permission of the editor of *Asian Folklore Studies*, Peter Knecht.

(continued on page 249)

CONTENTS

CONTENTS

Cleverness and Foolishness

INTRODUCTION

Stories give form to a people's hopes and dreams; they transmit values, they instruct, entertain, and unify the group to which they belong. Storytelling has long been one of the most fundamental ways of binding a group together, of passing traditions on to each new generation, of defining and reaffirming the shared history and beliefs of a people.

And likewise, hearing or reading stories of other times and places has always been a window into other people's worlds, a way to become familiar with what was before unknown, a path toward understanding what had once seemed beyond comprehension.

The countries of Pacific Asia—China, Japan, Korea, Vietnam, Thailand, Malaysia, Indonesia, and the Philippines—are among the most rapidly developing and economically powerful nations on earth, and yet their cultures are among the least understood by the rest of the world. Reading stories such as those in this collection may give some insight into the self-described identities of these cultures, and the values they hold. At the same time, because they treat fundamental, universal themes in compelling ways, they are entertaining in their own right.

Asia is home to many diverse cultures. Each region has its own indigenous culture, which may in turn be infused with aspects of one or more of the three dominant Asian cultures—Islamic from Western Asia, Indic from South Asia, and Chinese from East Asia. Within the regions represented in this volume, Chinese culture has greatly influenced Korea, Japan, and Vietnam, and to a lesser extent Indonesia and Malaysia. Hindu-Indic culture pervades Thailand and parts of Indonesia and Malaysia, while Islamic culture has left its mark in Indonesia and parts of the Philippines.

The existence of larger cultural spheres explains why many of the stories in this collection are part of the shared culture of several countries, not only of the country listed next to its title. The legend of the Herdsboy and the Weaving Maid, for example, is widely known in Korea, Japan, and Vietnam, as well as in China; and many of the animal stories from Indonesia and Malaysia are similar to traditional Indian stories, sometimes substituting local animals for those in the original tale. On the other hand, some stories, especially those about local spirits or the origins of local customs, appear to be unique to particular regions.

The six categories into which the stories are divided are arbitrary, devised solely for the convenience of grouping this particular set of stories, and are not meant to imply any intrinsic generic boundaries. Some of the stories of How Things Came to Be, for example, are also Myths or Legends or Animal Tales. Several of the Animal Tales differ from tales of Cleverness and Foolishness only in that animals instead of human beings are the main actors. Similarly, some stories of Magic Gifts and of Ghosts, Dreams, and the Supernatural are also Legends or Animal Tales or stories of Cleverness and Foolishness.

Some of the stories stem from ancient mythological traditions (for example, "The Sea Palace," from the Japanese *Kojiki*); some come from early works of history ("The River God's Wife," from Sima Qian's *Shi Ji*); some from literary collections ("The Painted Skin," from Pu Songling's *Liao Zhai Zhiyi*); and some from a long oral tradition ("Mouse-Deer Tales"). All the stories are well known within their cultures of origin, and they reveal the concerns and values of the people who tell and retell them.

Common concerns transcend cultural boundaries: the struggles between good and evil, wit and crude force, and mankind and the supernatural powers. Values which frequently emerge in the working out of such struggles include cleverness, loyalty, frugality, generosity, bravery, filial piety, and patience. Good usually triumphs in the end, but some stories of the supernatural leave one with the haunting fear that when dealing with otherworldly powers the usual rules do not apply.

But the stories speak for themselves. You are invited now to sample this collection, and through the stories visit the cultures that created them.

How Things Came To Be

Not long after children learn to speak they begin asking questions about why things are the way they are. Why is the sky blue? Why is ice cold? Where does fire go when it goes out? Why do cats chase mice? Adults too want answers. Why do rivers flow eastward (as most rivers in China do)? Why is the sea salty? Who made the first people, and why?

Many traditional stories are structured around answering such questions. Some of these stories become part of a people's religious faith or their understanding of their historical past. In other cases there is no question of belief—the stories simply entertain with bizarre or almost plausible accounts of how something might have happened, and the delight that these stories bring stems from their artful structure, not from any belief that the stories are true.

The stories presented in this section explain, among other things, how the earth was formed and people were made; why the sun is so bright; how the tiger got his stripes; how the mosquito came to be; and why the Da-Trang crabs endlessly scoop up sand.

The stories are of many different types, including ancient myth ("Pan Gu, Nuwa, and Gonggong") and local legend ("Da-Trang Crabs"). "The Salt-Grinding Millstones" combines the theme of a Magic Gift with a moral about the consequences of greed, then explains why the sea is salty. "The Sun and the Moon" contains a freestanding tale of children outwitting a tiger, remarkably similar in form and content to a European märchen or fairy tale, with two explanations added to the end almost as an afterthought. In this and several of the other stories in this group, the explanation bows to the plot of the story, illustrating the complexity of many traditional tales.

Pan Gu, Nuwa, and Gonggong
China

Long, long ago, before the heavens were separated from the earth, the world was an unformed mass shaped like an egg. Inside this egg was a man named Pan Gu, who grew larger and larger each day until he was ninety thousand *li* tall. He slept in the egg for eighteen thousand years, and then he woke up.

When Pan Gu opened his eyes he was surrounded by darkness, so he took an axe and with a mighty swing chopped the egg into two halves. One half rose upward to become Heaven, while the other sank down to become Earth. Pan Gu was afraid that Heaven and Earth would come together again, so he stood between them like a giant pillar, his feet on the Earth, and his shoulders holding up Heaven. After many eons had passed, Heaven and Earth grew so far apart they could never come together again, and Pan Gu, exhausted by his long effort, fell down and died.

His left eye became the sun, his right eye the moon, his body became mountains, and his blood rivers. The tiny hairs on his body became flowers and trees, his bones became metal and stones, and his beads of sweat became rain and pearls.

One day the goddess Nuwa came to the new world which Pan Gu had formed. She climbed the mountains and crossed the rivers, she looked at the flowers and the trees, but always she felt that something was lacking. As she gazed into a pool of water and saw her own reflection there she thought to herself, "I will make some living beings in my own image." Then she mixed some clay with water and carefully formed a figure out of the clay. When this figure was placed on the ground it came alive, and began to run and jump and shout. Nuwa gave it the name *Human*.

Then she carefully formed several other figures from the clay, and they all came to life. But the work took much time, and she began to tire of the task. So she took a rope, dipped it into a pool of mud, and flung it in all directions. Each of the drops that fell from the rope became a human too, though not as well formed as the first. The carefully formed figures became nobility, and the drops of mud became commoners, and that is why there are so many commoners and so few noble people in the world today.

Around this time, Gonggong, god of the waters, fought with Zhurong, the god of fire. Gonggong set out on a river raft to meet Zhurong, but though Gonggong was aided by fish, shrimp, and crabs, Zhurong proved more powerful, and burned all Gonggong's troops to death. Angry and ashamed at his defeat, Gonggong fled to the west, and in a terrible rage smashed into one of the four mountain pillars that support the sky. The force of his impact broke the pil-

17

lar, and a corner of the sky began to crumble. With the pillar broken, the western edge of the sky began to tilt downward to meet the earth, and the earth tilted upward to meet the sky. That is why the heavenly bodies flow toward the west, and the rivers of China flow toward the east.

The Sun and the Moon
Korea

Long, long ago there lived an old woman who had two children, a son and a daughter. One day she went to a neighboring village to work in a rich man's house. When she left to come back home, she was given a big wooden box containing buckwheat puddings. She carried it on her head, and hastened back to her waiting children. But on the way, as she passed a hill, she met a big tiger.

The tiger blocked her path, and opening its great red mouth asked, "Old woman, old woman! What is that you are carrying on your head?" The old woman replied fearlessly, "Do you mean this, Tiger? It is a box of buckwheat puddings that I was given at the rich man's house where I worked today." Then the tiger said, "Old woman, give me one. If you don't, I will eat you up." So she gave the tiger a buckwheat pudding, and it let her pass the hill.

When she came to the next hill the tiger appeared before her and asked her the same question, "Old woman, old woman, what have you got in that box you are carrying on your head?" And, thinking it was another tiger, she gave the same answer, "These are buckwheat puddings I was given at the rich man's house where I worked today." The tiger asked for one in the same way. And the old woman gave it a pudding from her box, and it went off into the forest.

The tiger then appeared several more times and made the same demand, and each time she gave it a pudding, until there were no more left in the box. So now she carried the empty box on her head, and she walked along swinging her arms at her sides. Then the tiger appeared again, and demanded a pudding. She explained that she had none left, saying, "Your friends ate all my buckwheat puddings. There is nothing at all left in my box." Thereupon she threw the box away. The tiger said, "What are those things swinging at your sides?" "This is my left arm, and this is my right arm," she replied. "Unless you give me one of them, I will eat you up," roared the tiger. So she gave it one of her arms, and it walked off with it. But not long afterwards it appeared in front of her again, and repeated its threats. So she gave it her other arm.

Now the old woman had lost all her puddings, her box, and even both her arms, but she still walked along the mountain road on her two legs. The greedy tiger barred her way once more and asked, "What is that, moving under your body?" She answered, "My legs, of course." The tiger then said, in a rather strange tone, "Oh, in that case, give me one of your legs, or I will eat you up." The old woman got very angry, and complained, "You greedy animal! Your friends ate all my puddings, and both my arms as well. Now you want my legs. However will I be able to get back to my home?" But the tiger would not listen to her, and persisted in its demand. "If you give me your left leg, you can still hop on your right leg, can't you?" So she had to take off her left leg, and throw it to the tiger, and then she set off homewards, hopping on her other leg. The tiger ran ahead of her, and barred her way again. "Old woman, old woman! Why are you hopping like that?" it asked. She shouted furiously, "You devil! You ate all my puddings, both my arms, and one of my legs. However can I go home if I lose my right leg too?" The tiger answered, "You can roll, can't you?" So she cut off her right leg, and gave it to the tiger. She set out to roll over and over along the road. Then the tiger rushed after her, and swallowed what was left of her in a single gulp.

Back at the old woman's home her two children waited till nightfall for her to return. Then they went inside and locked the door, and lay down hungry on the floor, for they did not know that a tiger had eaten their mother on her way home.

The cunning tiger dressed in the old woman's clothes, and put a white handkerchief on its head. Then, standing erect on its hind legs, it walked to the old woman's house and knocked at the door. It called to the two children, "My dears, you must be very hungry. Open the door. I have brought you some buckwheat puddings." But the children remembered the advice their mother had given them when she went out in the morning, "There are tigers about. Be very careful." They noticed that the voice sounded rather strange, and so they did not open the door, and said, "Mother, your voice sounds rather strange. What has happened to you?" So the tiger disguised its voice and said, "Don't be alarmed. Mother is back. I have spent the day spreading barley to dry on mats, and the sparrows kept flying down to eat it, so that I had to shout loudly at them all day long to drive them away. So I have got rather hoarse." The children were not convinced, and asked again, "Then, Mother, please put your arm in through the hole in the door, and let us see it." The tiger put one of its forepaws in the hole in the door. The children touched it and said, "Mother, why is your arm so rough and hairy?" So the tiger explained, "I was washing clothes, and I starched them with rice paste. That must have made my arm rough." But the children peeped out through the hole in the door, and were surprised to see a tiger there in the darkness. So they slipped quietly out the back door, climbed a tall tree, and hid among the branches.

The tiger waited for a while, but as it got no further reply from inside, it broke into the house, and searched in vain for the children. It came out in a furious temper, and rushed round the house with terrible roars, till it came to an old well underneath the tree. It looked down at the water, and there saw the reflections of the two children. So it forced a smile and tried to scoop up the reflections, and said in a gentle voice, "Oh, my poor children. You have fallen into the well. I haven't got a bamboo basket, or even a grass one. How can I save you?" The children watched the tiger's antics from above, and could not help bursting out laughing. Hearing their laughter it looked up, and saw them high in the tree. It asked in a kindly voice, "How did you get up there? That's very dangerous. You might fall into the well. I must get you down. Tell me how you got up so high." The children replied, "Go to the neighbors and get some sesame oil. Smear it on the trunk and climb up."

So the stupid tiger went to the house next door and got some sesame oil and smeared it thickly on the trunk and tried to climb up. But of course the oil made the tree very slippery. So the tiger asked again, "My dear children. You are very clever, aren't you? However did you get up there so easily, right to the top? Tell me the truth." This time they answered innocently, "Go and borrow an axe from the neighbors. Then you can cut footholds on the trunk." So the tiger went and borrowed an axe from the house next door, and, cutting steps in the tree, began to climb up.

The children now thought that they would not be able to escape from the tiger, and in great terror prayed to the God of Heaven. "Oh God, please save us. If you are willing, please send us the Heavenly Iron Chain. But if you mean us to die, send down the Rotten Straw Rope!" At once a strong Iron Chain came gently down from Heaven to them, so that they could climb up without difficulty.

When the tiger reached the top of the tree the children were gone. It wanted to follow them, so it too began to pray, but in opposite terms, because it was very afraid that it might be punished for its misdeeds. "Oh God of Heaven, if you would save me, send down the Rotten Straw Rope, I beg of you. But if you mean me to die, please send down the Heavenly Iron Chain." By praying in this way, it hoped that the Iron Chain would come down, and not the Straw Rope, for it expected that as a punishment it would received the opposite of what it had prayed for. But the gods are straightforward, and always willing to save lives by answering prayers directly, and so it was the Rotten Straw Rope that came down after all. The tiger seized the rope, and began to climb up it, for in the darkness it could not see that it was not the chain. When it got a little way up, the rope broke, and so it fell down to the ground. It crashed down in a field of broom-corn, where it died crushed and broken, its body pierced through by the sharp stems of the corn. From that day, it is said, the leaves of broom-corn have been covered with blood-red spots.

The two children lived peacefully in the Heavenly Kingdom, until one day the Heavenly King said to them, "We do not allow anyone to sit here and idle away the time. So I have decided on duties for you. The boy shall be the Sun, to light the world of men, and the girl shall be the Moon, to shine by night." Then the girl answered, "Oh King, I am not familiar with the night. It would be better for me not to be the Moon." So the King made her the Sun instead, and made her brother the Moon.

It is said that when she became the Sun, people used to gaze up at her in the sky. But she was a modest girl, and greatly embarrassed by this. So she shone brighter and brighter, so that it was impossible to look at her directly. And that is why the sun is so bright, that her womanly modesty might be forever respected.

The Salt-Grinding Millstones
Japan

In a certain place there were two brothers. The older brother was a very unpleasant fellow, but the younger brother was very good and intelligent.

The older brother wanted to marry his younger brother off as an adopted husband as soon as possible so that he would not have to worry about him, but the younger brother wanted to remain single and had no desire to go somewhere and become an adopted husband.

After a while, however, he did take a wife. They borrowed a hut from someone and lived in it. When winter came there was less work than he had expected, and they were in distress. Then the last day of the year came, and he went to his older brother's house to borrow one *sho* of rice. His older brother said, "What is this! Is there anyone stupid enough to have no rice to eat at the year's end feast? After all, it comes but once a year! And even worse than that, you have gone and gotten married. You can go somewhere else and tell your story." And he absolutely refused to give him anything. Without a word, the younger brother left the older brother's house.

He was crossing the mountain when he met an old man with a long beard who was picking up firewood. "Where are you going?" asked the old man.

"Tonight is the last night of the year, but we have no rice to offer to the *Toshigama* [Year Deity], and so I am just walking about, going nowhere in particular," replied the young man.

"Well, that is too bad. Here, I will give you this, you may take it with you," and he gave him a tiny *manju* dumpling made from wheat flour. Then he added, "Take this *manju* and go over there to the temple of the deity of the forest. Behind the temple there is a hole in the ground. There are some *kobito* [little people] who live in that hole; they will ask you to give them the *manju,* but you must tell them that you will not exchange it for money or anything but a pair of millstones. The *kobito* dearly love *manju.*"

The young man thanked the old man and went to the temple in the middle of the forest as he had been told. He looked behind the temple and saw that, sure enough, there was a hole there. He went down into the hole and found a large number of *kobito,* who were making a great deal of noise. He wondered what they were doing; when he looked closely, he could see that they were trying to climb up a reed stalk but were falling off and trying again, then falling off and trying again. He thought this very strange and said, "Here, I'll help you," and picking them up, he soon had put them where they were trying to go. The *kobito* were very happy and said in awe, "Oh, what a huge man you are; you are really strong!" Just then they noticed the wheat flour *manju* that he was carrying. "Oh, oh, what a nice looking thing that is you're carrying; how unusual it looks! Please let us have it, will you?" and they spread out some gold in front of him.

As the younger brother had been instructed by the old man, he said, "No, I don't want gold. I will trade this for your millstones." The *kobito* were troubled. "There are no other millstones in the world like these; they are our treasure. But there is nothing else to do; we will trade them to you." And so they handed them over to him.

The young man gave the *kobito* the *manju,* and taking the tiny millstones, he climbed out of the hole. Just as he got outside, he heard a voice as small as a mosquito's calling, "You're killing me, you're killing me!" He looked around carefully and found that one of the *kobito* was caught between the supports of his high clogs. He carefully took him out and put him back in the hole.

He set off again and came to where the old man had been on the mountain pass. The old man was there again. He said, "Oh, did you get the millstones? If you turn those millstones to the right, anything you want will come out. If you turn them to the left, they will stop."

The younger brother happily returned home. When he got home, his wife had grown very tired of waiting. "Today is the celebration of the last day of the year, and where have you been?" she complained. "Did you go over to your brother's place and get something to eat?"

"It's all right. Hurry, spread out a straw mat here," he said. His wife spread out a mat, and he put the millstones on it. "Make rice, make rice," he said, turning the stones. Rice came pouring out in a stream, *zoko zoko,* one bushel and then another. Next he said, "Make salmon," and two salted salmon, then three, came sliding out, *hyoko hyoko.* After everything necessary for their feast had been provided by the millstones, they had a very happy year's end feast; then they went to sleep.

The next morning was New Year's Day. The young man said, "Since were are now so rich, it is no fun living in a little hut like this; make us a new house." And he turned the millstones. A splendid mansion appeared. Then he made many storehouses, a long house for servants, a horse barn, and seven horses, all from the millstone.

"Make *mochi.* Make *sake,*" he said, turning the millstones, and *mochi* and *sake* appeared. He invited all his relatives in the neighborhood and made a great celebration. The villagers were very surprised, and all came to the feast. His older brother was astounded. He thought it so strange that he could not restrain himself but went around here and there, all about the house, trying to see how it had been done.

The younger brother thought that he would make some cakes and candies to give the villagers as presents, so he went into the next room and said, "Make sweetmeats, make sweetmeats," and turned the millstones. While he was doing this, the older brother peeked in and saw what he was doing. "Aha, now I see, it is all done by those millstones," he said.

When the feast was over, the villagers all returned home. The younger brother and his wife went to bed. After they had gone to sleep, the older brother crept silently into the next room and stole the millstones, then fled. He also took some *mochi* and some sweetmeats. Taking everything he had gotten, he ran until he came to the seashore. Luckily there was a boat tied up there. He jumped in and pushed off. He decided that he would take the millstones to someplace where he could become a very rich man. He began to row the boat with all his might and rowed a good way out to sea, when he began to get hungry. He ate the *mochi* and the sweet cakes and candies, but with so much sweet stuff, he felt hungry for salt. There was none in the boat so he decided that this would be a good chance to try the millstones. He said, "Well, well, make some salt, make some salt," and he turned the millstones. Immediately, salt began to pour, *doshi doshi,* from the stones. He soon thought that he had enough, but he did not know how to make the stones stop. He became frightened, but the stones kept on turning and making salt until the boat was full; then finally it sank, and he sank with it, down into the sea.

Since there was no one to turn the millstones toward the

left, they are still at the bottom of the sea, turning and turning, *guru guru,* and making salt, and that is why the sea is so salty.

The Twelve Animals of the Zodiac
China

Long ago, people did not know how to keep track of the months and years, so they asked the Jade Emperor to help them with this task. The Jade Emperor thought that using the names of twelve animals to name the years would make it easier for people to remember them. But there were so many animals in the world, how could he choose just twelve?

The Jade Emperor decided that on his birthday he would have a contest among all the animals to see which could cross the river the fastest. The first twelve animals to cross the river and reach the finish line would become the twelve animals of the zodiac, after whom the years would be named.

The news of the contest spread far and wide, and all the animals came to test their skills. At that time the cat and the rat were best of friends. They ate together, they slept together, and in a word, they were as inseparable as glue and lacquer.

The rat said, "I should very much like to be first, and stand at the head of the zodiac, but I am too small and not much good at swimming."

The cat said, "Since we are small and not very fast, we should get an early start. I have heard that the ox gets up at the crack of dawn. Why don't we ask the ox to wake us up early on the day of the contest, and maybe if we go with him we will have a chance."

The rat clapped his paws and squeaked, "Yes, yes! Let's do that!"

On the Jade Emperor's birthday, before the dawn began to break, before the rooster began to crow, the kindly ox came to waken the cat and the rat. Seeing how sleepy they were he said, "I don't think you'll get very far, very fast when you're still half asleep. Why don't you just hop on my back and ride with me?"

The cat and the rat gladly settled down on the ox's broad, warm back, and soon were fast asleep again. When they finally woke up the sky was just growing light, and the ox had already reached the river. The cat lazily yawned and said, "As soon as we cross the river we will be almost at the finish line. It looks like we three will be the first across."

"Yes, you came up with a clever plan," said the rat, all the while thinking that it was all well and good that the three of them would be first across the river, but how could he make sure that at the very end he would be ahead of the cat and the ox?

The selfish rat hit upon a devious plan. When they had reached the middle of the river he said to the cat, "Look, Brother Cat, at the fine landscape on the far shore!" When the cat stood on tiptoe to gaze into the distance, the rat gave him a push and he fell into the river.

The ox felt that the weight on his back had grown lighter, but when he looked back he saw the horse and the tiger and other animals gaining on him, so he forgot about the cat and the rat and swam as fast as he could toward the far shore. The clever rat, meanwhile, had hidden itself in the ox's ear. When the ox reached the shore he felt something jump out of his ear, and when he stopped a moment to see what it was, the rat scurried to the goal line and finished first.

The Jade Emperor was surprised to see the rat had finished first, and said to him, "Mister Rat, I know you can't swim, and you don't run very fast, so how is it that you finished first?" The rat replied, "I may be little, but I'm smart! Of course I came in first!"

Soon the ox came lumbering up, angry at the rat for the trick he had played. Close behind him was the tiger, who raced to the finish line dripping wet, roaring, "I'm first, I'm first!" "No, I was first!" squeaked the rat. "You think you are so fine, because you are so strong, but to get ahead you have to be clever like me!" So the tiger and the rat began to squabble.

Suddenly there was a great whirlwind, and a dragon swooped down from the sky, but before he could alight, a rabbit, who had caught a ride on the tiger's back, hopped in front of him, winning fourth place. The dragon could fly, so he should have come in first, and the Jade Emperor asked him what had detained him.

"I would have been here earlier," said the dragon, "but I had to go make it rain in one of the eastern counties, and that delayed me a bit." Dragons, as everyone knows, are the creatures in charge of rain, and being a very responsible dragon he always put duty before pleasure.

Suddenly hoofbeats could be heard, and in the clouds of dust on the road one could make out a horse, sheep, monkey, rooster, and dog running with all their might. The horse was in front. Just as he was about to reach the finish line he heard a voice saying, "I was here first!" He looked around and could see no one, but looking again he discovered a snake in the grass. The snake's arrival caused a commotion, and the rat and the rabbit immediately hid out of sight.

"What number am I?" asked the horse, with a loud whinny. "Number seven, not bad," said the tiger.

Soon the sheep, monkey, and rooster arrived. "How is it

that you came together?" asked the rat. "We all were floating on the same old log," said the sheep, "and we helped one another row the log across." Then the sound of barking signaled the dog's arrival. He would have been there sooner, but he had stopped to play in the river. That made eleven.

The twelfth to arrive was the pig. "How is it that the pig, who is usually so lazy, made it across?" the animals asked each other. "Is there anything here to eat? Perhaps a banquet for the winners?" asked the pig, causing the other animals to burst out laughing.

Then the Jade Emperor announced the winners. "The twelve animals of the zodiac will be: Rat, Ox, Tiger, Rabbit, Dragon, Snake, Horse, Sheep . . ." But before he could finish, the soaking wet cat came limping up to the finish line, crying, "What number am I? What number am I?"

The Jade Emperor replied, "You are too late. You are not on the list." When the cat heard this he shouted, "It's all that sneaky rat's fault! He will pay for this! I am going to eat him up!"

The Jade Emperor tried to stop the cat, but the cat would not be stopped, and, claws extended, it lunged at the rat, who scurried behind the Jade Emperor's robes.

To this day the cat and the rat remain mortal enemies, and the rat, ashamed of the way he won first place in the zodiac, hides all day in dark corners and will only come out at night.

Half-Child
Indonesia

The first man and woman lived by a river, on whose banks they had a garden. A boy was born to them, but later, when a second child was about to be brought into the world, a great rain and flood came and washed away half of the garden, whereupon the woman cursed the rain, the result of her malediction being that when the child was born, it was only half a human being and had but one eye, one arm, and one leg.

When Half-Child had grown up, he said to his mother, "Alas, what shall I do, so that I may be like my brother, who has two arms and two legs?"

Determining to go to the great deity in the upper world and beg him to make him whole, he climbed up and laid his request before the god, who, after some discussion, agreed to help him, telling him to bathe in a pool which he showed him, and at the same time cautioning him not to go into the water if he saw anyone else bathing. Half-Child went to the pool, found no one else there, and after bathing came out transformed to his proper shape and made very handsome.

Returning to his home, he found his brother eating his dinner, and the latter said to him, "Well, brother, you look very beautiful!" "Yes," said Half-Child, "the deity granted me to be even as you are." Then his elder brother asked, "Is the god far away?" and the other replied, "No, he is not far, for I was able to reach him easily."

The elder brother at once went up to see the divinity, and when asked why he had come, he said that he wished to be made as handsome as his younger brother. The deity replied, "No, you are now just as you ought to be, and must remain so." But since the other would not be satisfied, at length the god said, "Well, go to that pool there and bathe; but you must not do so unless you see the image of a dog in it, in which case you must bathe with a piece of white cloth tied round your neck."

So the elder brother went to the pool, tied a piece of cloth around his neck, and bathed, and behold! he was turned into a dog with a white mark around his throat. When he returned to this world he found his brother, Half-Child, at dinner. "Alas!" said the younger brother, "I told you not to go, but you would do so, and now see what has become of you!" And he added, "Here, my brother, you must always remain under my table and eat what falls from it."

How the Tiger Got His Stripes
Vietnam

This story took place in prehistoric times, when animals still had the power of speech.

A young farmer had just stopped plowing his rice paddy. It was noon, and he sat down to eat his lunch in the shade of a banana plant near his land.

Not far away his water buffalo was grazing along the grass-covered dikes enclosing the rice fields. After the meal the farmer reclined and observed the stout beast which was chewing quietly. From time to time it would chase away the obnoxious flies with a vigorous swing of its massive head.

Suddenly the great beast became alarmed; the wind carried the odor of a dangerous animal. The buffalo rose to its feet, and awaited the arrival of the enemy.

With the speed of lightning, a tiger sprang into the clearing.

"I have not come as an enemy," he said. "I only wish to have something explained. I have been watching you every day from the edge of the forest, and I have observed the strange spectacle of your common labor with the man. That man, that small and vertical being, who has neither great strength nor sharp vision, nor even a keen sense of smell, has been able to keep you in bondage and work you for his profit. You are actually ten times heavier than he, much stronger, and more hardened to heavy labor. Yet he rules you. What is the source of his magic power?"

"To tell the truth," said the buffalo, "I know nothing about all that. I only know I shall never be freed of his power, for he has a talisman he calls wisdom."

"I must ask him about that," said the tiger, "because, you see, if I could get this wisdom I would have even greater power over the other animals. Instead of having to conceal myself and spring on them unawares, I could simply order them to remain motionless. I could choose from among all the animals, at my whim and fancy, the most delicious meats."

"Well!" replied the startled buffalo. "Why don't you ask the farmer about his wisdom."

The tiger decided to approach the farmer.

"Mr. Man," he said, "I am big, strong, and quick but I want to be more. I have heard it said that you have something called wisdom which makes it possible for you to rule over all the animals. Can you transfer this wisdom to me? It would be of great value to me in my daily search for food."

"Unfortunately," replied the man, "I have left my wisdom at home. I never bring it with me to the fields. But if you like, I will go there for it."

"May I accompany you?" asked the tiger, delighted with what he had just heard.

"No, you had better remain here," replied the farmer, "if the villagers see you with me they may become alarmed and perhaps beat you to death. Wait here. I will find what you need and return."

And the farmer took a few steps, as if to set off homeward. But then he turned around and with wrinkled brow addressed the tiger.

"I am somewhat disturbed by the possibility that during my absence you might be seized with the desire to eat my buffalo. I have great need of it in my daily work. Who would repay me for such a loss?"

The tiger did not know what to say.

The farmer continued: "If you consent, I will tie you to a tree; then my mind will be free."

The tiger wanted the mysterious wisdom very much—so much, in fact, that he was willing to agree to anything. He permitted the farmer to pass ropes round his body and to tie him to the trunk of a big tree.

The farmer went home and gathered a great armload of dry straw. He returned to the big tree and placed the straw under the tiger and set it on fire.

"Behold my wisdom!" he shouted at his unfortunate victim, as the flames encircled the tiger and burned him fiercely.

The tiger roared so loudly that the neighboring trees trembled. He raged and pleaded, but the farmer would not untie him.

Finally the fire burned through the ropes and he was able to free himself from cremation. He bounded away into the forest, howling with pain.

In time his wounds healed, but he was never able to rid himself of the long black stripes of the ropes which the flames had seared into his flesh.

The Mosquito
Vietnam

Ngoc Tam, a modest farmer, had married Nhan Diep. The two young people were poor but in excellent health, and they seemed destined to enjoy the happiness of a simple rural life. The husband worked in the paddy and cultivated a small field of mulberry trees, and the wife engaged in raising silkworms.

But Nhan Diep was a coquette at heart. She was lazy, and dreamed of luxury and pleasures. She was also clever enough to hide her desires and ambitions from her husband, whose love was genuine, but neither demanding nor discerning. He supposed his wife to be content with her lot and happy in her daily chores. Ngoc Tam toiled diligently, hoping to ease their poverty and improve their station in life.

Suddenly Nhan Diep was carried away by death. Ngoc Tam was plunged into such deep sorrow that he would not leave his wife's body and opposed its burial.

One day, after having sold his possessions, he embarked in a sampan with the coffin and sailed away.

One morning he found himself at the foot of a fragrant, green hill which perfumed the countryside.

He went ashore and discovered a thousand rare flowers and orchards of trees laden with the most varied kinds of fruit.

There he met an old man who supported himself with a bamboo cane. His hair was white as cotton and his face wrinkled and sunburned, but under his blond eyelashes his eyes sparkled like those of a young boy. By this last trait, Ngoc Tam recognized the genie of medicine, who traveled throughout the world on his mountain, Thien Thai, to teach his science to the men of the earth and to alleviate their ills.

Ngoc Tam threw himself at the genie's feet.

Then the genie spoke to him: "Having learned of your virtues, Ngoc Tam, I have stopped my mountain on your route. If you wish, I will admit you to the company of my disciples."

Ngoc Tam thanked him profusely but said that he desired only to live with his wife. He had never thought of any life other than the one he would lead with her, and he begged the genie to bring her back to life.

The genie looked at him with kindness mixed with pity and said, "Why do you cling to this world of bitterness and gall? The rare joys of this life are only a snare. How foolish you were to entrust your destiny to a weak and inconstant being! I want to grant your wishes, but I fear that you will regret it later."

Then, on the genie's order, Ngoc Tam opened the coffin; he cut the tip of his finger and let three drops of blood fall on Nhan Diep's body. The latter opened her eyes slowly, as if awakening from a deep sleep. Then her faculties quickly returned.

"Do not forget your obligations," the genie said to her. "Remember your husband's devotion. May you both be happy."

On the voyage home Ngoc Tam rowed day and night, eager to reach his native land again. One evening he went ashore in a certain port to buy provisions. During his absence a large ship came alongside the wharf, and the owner, a rich merchant, was struck by Nhan Diep's beauty. He entered into conversation with her and invited her to have refreshments aboard his vessel. As soon as she was aboard, he gave the order to cast off and sailed away.

Ngoc Tam searched an entire month for his wife before locating her aboard the merchant's vessel.

She answered his questions without the least hesitation, but had grown accustomed to her new life. It satisfied her completely and she refused to return home with him. Then for the first time, Ngoc Tam saw her in her true light. Suddenly he felt all love for her vanish, and he no longer desired her return.

"You are free," he said to her. "Only return to me the three drops of blood that I gave to bring you back to life. I do not want to leave the least trace of myself in you."

Happy to be set free so cheaply, Nhan Diep took a knife and cut the tip of her finger. But, as soon as the blood began to flow, she turned pale and sank to the ground. An instant later she was dead.

Even so, the lighthearted frivolous woman could not resign herself to leave this world forever. She returned in the form of a small insect and followed Ngoc Tam relentlessly, in order to steal the three drops of blood from him, which would restore her to human life. Day and night she worried her former husband, buzzing around him incessantly, protesting her innocence, and begging his pardon. Later, she received the name of *mosquito*. Unfortunately for us, her race has multiplied many times.

The Da-Trang Crabs
Vietnam

Every morning of the world, just after dawn had fingered the sky, Da-Trang the hunter left his straw hut, mounted his horse, and rode deep into the forest with his bow and arrows. He never returned until evening, when he fetched home whatever animals he had killed. Being a skillful huntsman, he never came home empty-handed.

One day he happened to pass a pagoda near which he saw two black serpents spotted with white. At first he recoiled instinctively in fear, but, since they did him no harm, he grew quickly accustomed to their presence. Eventually, since he made a practice of following the same route each day and saw the serpents frequently, he came to understand that these were serpent-spirits. To honor them, Da-Trang formed the habit of placing an offering of game at the foot of the altar in the pagoda whenever he passed.

One day, while approaching the pagoda, Da-Trang heard a great rustling of leaves and beating of grass. Following the sounds, he arrived in time to see the two black-and-white serpents under attack by a yellow serpent that was much, much larger than they. Quick as a thought, Da-Trang seized his bow, drew on the attacker, and wounded him in the head, causing him to flee away. One of the two black serpents rushed after in pursuit, but the other, seriously wounded in the encounter, soon died. Da-Trang buried it carefully behind the pagoda.

That very night a spirit summoned Da-Trang to a pile of stones outside his hut and said to him, "Today you saved me from the fangs of my enemy, and then you paid the final respects and honors to my poor wife. Here is proof of my gratitude."

Then, while Da-Trang stood watching, the spirit again assumed serpent shape. The serpent opened wide its mouth and let fall a pearl that gleamed in the darkness of the night.

Da-Trang had always heard it said that the possession of a pearl from a serpent-spirit gave the owner the ability to understand the language of animals. So, next morning, before leaving to hunt, he placed the pearl in his mouth, determined to put this adage to the test.

Scarcely had he entered the forest than he heard a voice which seemed to descend from the top of a tall tree nearby:

To the right, at two hundred paces, who sees a deer?
To the right, at two hundred paces, who sees it?

It was a raven counseling the hunter in this fashion.

Da-Trang followed the raven's advice, and when he had felled his prey, the bird cried out, "Don't forget my pay! Don't forget to pay me!"

Da-Trang surmised that just as he could understand the raven, the raven could understand him. So he put the question, "What do you want?"

The bird replied at once, "The entrails! Only the entrails!"

At once Da-Trang paid his debt to the bird.

Next day the raven was there again, and gave the hunter some more valuable information from his perch. Thus the hunter and the bird gradually formed a sort of association. And Da-Trang, grateful for the fine game he was taking, always took care to place his feathered partner's share of the kill in a convenient spot.

But one day this share was stolen by some animal before the raven arrived to claim it. The bird thought that Da-Trang had forgotten to reward him, and he went directly to Da-Trang's home to complain. The hunter denied the accusation, of course, and protested his innocence. The partners wound up quarreling. The raven began to hurl insults at Da-Trang, who became enraged, and, in his fury, let fly a poisoned arrow.

The bird swerved and avoided being struck. But he picked up the arrow at the spot where it fell, and clutching it in his beak, he flew away at full speed, crying, "Revenge! Revenge! I'm going to get revenge!"

Several days later, Da-Trang was arrested. A poisoned arrow marked with his name had been found in the body of a drowned man. Despite his vigorous protests, Da-Trang was thrown into prison.

There the jailer soon became exceedingly amazed at his prisoner's strange behavior. He heard him laughing and talking, even though he knew the man was all alone in his cell. Naturally, the jailer thought Da-Trang had taken leave of his senses. But Da-Trang, who still carried the pearl in his mouth, was simply talking with all the little animals in his cell, begging mosquitoes and other insects and bugs not to bite him, or listening to their evaluation of the prisoners who had preceded him in this cell.

Once he surprised a conversation between two sparrows who were boasting about how they had emptied several of the royal granaries that were poorly guarded. Da-Trang immediately demanded to see the prison warden and reported this tale. At first skeptical, the warden checked, found the story to be true, and was convinced that Da-Trang had not imagined the whole thing.

A little later, some ants that were hastily transporting their eggs and supplies to higher places were questioned by Da-Trang about this rapid movement. They revealed to him that a great flood was imminent.

Alerted to this by the imprisoned huntsman, the warden hurriedly carried the prophecy to the king himself. The ruler immediately ordered that all necessary precautions be taken. Three days later the waters of the great river rose rapidly and overflowed, inundating vast areas.

The king then summoned Da-Trang into his presence. From his lips, the ruler learned the whole truth, from the story of the serpents up to the vengeance of the raven. The king examined the magic pearl. Marveling, he saw in his mind innumerable projects that he could assist with it, all of them in the public interest. He hoped as well to discover for his own information more of nature's secrets and other wonders unknown to the rest of mankind. Yet he did not want to deprive Da-Trang of his pearl. So he kept him close at hand and consulted often with him, urging him to repeat all that he heard from the animal world.

Thus did Da-Trang live happily, near his king and close to animals of every species, small ones, big ones, those that walk, those that crawl, those that fly. In the beginning the king took a deep interest in these conversations and devoted a good share of his time to them. He observed that animals are not nearly so simple as one might believe and that men are wrong to slight them or disregard them or feel too superior to them. For animals resemble humans, strangely, and each species forms a world of its own, with its own absurdities, its own cruelties, and its own miseries, quite comparable to those that affect human society.

But eventually the king grew tired of listening to animal talk, and in hope of new discoveries, he led Da-Trang in long walks by the sea. There they questioned the most varied types of fish, but there, too, really interesting conversations were rare. And the king became convinced that, like the animals of the land, the denizens of the deep spoke most often to say nothing, or only to do damage with their words.

On a beautiful spring morning, leaving Da-Trang to rest in the shade, the king followed with his eyes the debates of a school of dolphins. The wind wrinkled the calm surface of the sparkling sea and made the dazzling grains of golden sand twinkle.

Suddenly something roused Da-Trang from his reverie. Cupping his ear in his hand, he leaned over the water. A cuttlefish was swimming beside the royal barge and singing joyfully,

> Cloud, white cloud
> That swims, paddling slowly
> In the blue waters of the sky . . .

It was so ridiculous, so funny, this cuttlefish singing this absurd song while rocking through the water in rhythm to the melody, that Da-Trang burst into laughter. As he did so, the pearl slipped from his mouth and fell into the sea.

The sorrow of the king at this turn of events was keen, but it could not touch Da-Trang's despair. They marked the spot where the mishap had occurred and summoned the best divers in the kingdom. But, as might have been anticipated, the search was quite in vain.

Though the king felt sincere regret, his sorrow did not last, for he had his own pursuits and other distractions. But Da-Trang himself remained inconsolable. Day and night, he could think of nothing but his tragic loss. No longer could he take interest in anything, and, despite the solicitude of his monarch, who remained ever mindful of the services Da-Trang had rendered him, he wept endlessly for the irreplaceable pearl.

Finally his mind went to pieces under the impact of his grief, and he conceived the irrational notion of filling up the sea in order to find his precious magic pearl again. So he assembled a whole army of workmen who scattered hundreds of barrows of sand daily on the beach. At first the king indulged him in this whim. But after a time he felt he had to stop the senseless act.

Alas! Da-Trang wasted away and died without ever fully recovering his reason. He asked to be buried in the same spot where he had attempted to fill in the ocean, his head facing toward the sea that had ravished his treasure from him.

When you are at the edge of the sea, go to the beach in the early morning, at ebb tide, and you will observe numberless small heaps of sand. These are the work of Da-Trang Crabs, as they are called, which swarm about your feet and then, at the slightest alarm, dart into their holes in the sand. Using their claws, they quickly pull the sand into the hole after them. But then a single wave comes along and destroys all their work in a second. Undaunted, the crabs then start all over again to scoop and roll up more sand against the next onslaught of the waters. This goes on endlessly.

So it is said that the tireless, restless soul of Da-Trang passed into this species of crab and that, unable even in death to forget the loss of his magic pearl, he still continues his vain effort to fill up the ocean.

Animal Tales

The combination of familiarity and strangeness we recognize in animals makes them intriguing subjects for stories. People tell stories in which animals behave almost like human beings, with qualities such as cleverness, meanness, cruelty, vanity, and stupidity. Yet animals also belong to a world apart, a world of unknown natural forces. Fear and wonder about this side of animals emerge in stories about their supernatural powers.

Among the most popular animal stories worldwide are those centered around a trickster figure—a clever animal who outwits bigger or more powerful animals. One reason for their widespread appeal is that these stories give form to the universal desire of the weak and powerless (which includes everyone, for there are always forces stronger than even the strongest men) to triumph over the cruel forces which oppress them.

In Asia the villain of such stories is often a tiger, though it may also be a crocodile or other predator, and the hero is usually a small but clever animal such as a rabbit or monkey. The tiny mouse-deer, or *kantjil,* is the subject of many Indonesian trickster stories. He is the hero in the "Mouse-Deer Tales" collected here. The monkey in "The Jelly-fish and the Monkey," and the hare in "The Old Tiger and the Hare" are typical tricksters. In an interesting variation, both main characters in "The Turtle and the Monkey" are trickster figures, but in this case the turtle wins out in the end.

Another type of animal tale centers around an animal's magical power to transform itself into diverse shapes. In popular Japanese stories the fox and the badger have the ability to assume the shape of other animals, people, or even artifacts such as statues, temples, bridges, or teakettles, and they often use their disguises to try to trick people.

Sometimes they win; sometimes they lose, and—since human beings and not tigers are the ones being tricked—these stories create a disturbing feeling of vulnerability not found in the cheerful animal-vs.-animal stories. "Three Fox Stories," "The Crackling Mountain," and "The Miraculous Tea-kettle" are Japanese stories built around this theme. Additional stories of supernatural animals interacting with human beings, even marrying them, can be found in the section on "Ghosts, Dreams, and the Supernatural" later in this collection.

Two miscellaneous animal tales presented here are "The Mouse Lord Chooses a Bridegroom" and "The Locust, the Ant, and the Kingfisher." The former is something like an elaborate riddle, and the latter involves some minor trickery and some explanations of how things came to be.

Mouse-Deer Tales
Indonesia

One day the mouse-deer was resting quietly when he heard a tiger approaching. Fearing for his life, he took a large leaf and began to fan a pile of dung which happened to lie nearby. When the tiger came up it was overcome by curiosity and asked the mouse-deer what he was doing. "This is food which belongs to the king. I am guarding it," the mouse-deer replied.

The tiger, being very hungry, at once wished to be allowed to eat the royal food, but the mouse-deer refused for a long time, advising him not to touch it and saying that it would be wrong to betray his trust. But at last he agreed to let the tiger have his way, if he would promise to wait before eating it until he, the mouse-deer, had gone, for in this way he would escape blame.

No sooner said than done; when the mouse-deer had reached a safe distance, he called back to the tiger, "You may begin now." The tiger hungrily seized what he thought was a delicious morsel, only to find it was stinking dung. Furious at the trick played upon him by the little mouse-deer, he hurried after the fugitive to get his revenge.

The mouse-deer meanwhile had found a venomous snake which lay coiled up asleep. Sitting by the snake he awaited the tiger's arrival, and when the latter came up raging in pursuit, he told him that he had only himself to blame, since he had been warned not to eat the food. "But," he said, "you must keep quiet, for I am guarding the king's girdle. You must not come near it, because it is full of magic power."

The tiger's curiosity and desire being, of course, only stimulated by all this, he insisted that he be allowed to try on the precious girdle, to which the mouse-deer yielded with apparent reluctance, again warning him to be careful and, as before, saying that the tiger must first let him get safely away, in order that no guilt might fall on him. When the mouse-deer had run off, the tiger seized what he thought was the magic girdle, only to be bitten by the snake.

◆

One day the mouse-deer was going out fishing when the tortoise, the deer, the elephant, and several other animals asked to be allowed to go with him. He agreed, and so large a catch was secured that the party resolved to smoke a portion to preserve it. The elephant remained behind the next day to watch the drying fish, but while he was on guard there came a great crashing in the forest, and presently a huge giant appeared, a forest demon, who calmly stole the fish, ate them, and walked away without the elephant daring to stop him.

When the fishermen returned, they were much disturbed over the loss of their fish, but as they again had a large supply, they left another of the party on guard the next day. Once more the giant came and ate all the fish. This continued until all the animals had had their turn except the mouse-deer. The other animals laughed at the tiny fellow's boast that he would catch and kill the thief.

As soon as the others had gone, the mouse-deer got four strong posts and drove them into the ground, after which he collected some rattan and began to plait four large strong rings. Before long the giant came crashing through the forest, but just as he was about to take the fish, he saw the mouse-deer, who kept busily at work and paid not the slightest attention to the intruder. Overcome by curiosity, the demon asked what the mouse-deer was doing, and the latter replied that his friends suffered much from pains in the back, so that he was preparing a remedy for them.

"That is interesting," said the giant, "for I, too, suffer much from pains in my back. I wish you would cure me." "All right," said the mouse-deer. "Go over there and lie down, put your elbows close to your sides, and draw up your knees, and I will massage you and apply the cure."

The giant at once complied, and the tricky mouse-deer, quickly slipping the strong rattan rings over the demon's arms, legs, and body, fastened them securely to the great posts. In vain did the giant struggle to get free, but the rattan bonds could not be broken, so that when the fishermen came back, they found the mouse-deer sitting quietly beside his captive, whereupon they at once attacked the monster who had been so neatly trapped and beat him to death.

◆

One day the mouse-deer wished to cross a river which he was unable to wade or swim because it was in a flood. So, standing on the bank, he called for the crocodiles, saying that the king had given the command that they should be counted. The crocodiles came in great numbers and by the mouse-deer's directions arranged themselves in a row extending from bank to bank. Then the mouse-deer jumped from one to the other calling out, "one," "two," "three," pretending to count them, until he reached the opposite bank, from whence he derided them for their stupidity.

Resolving to be avenged, one of the crocodiles bided his time, and when the mouse-deer later came to the river to drink, he seized one of the mouse-deer's legs in his mouth. The mouse-deer calmly picked up a branch and called out, "That is not my leg; that is a stick of wood. My foot is here." The crocodile then let go and snapped at the branch, thinking it was really the mouse-deer's leg. This gave the needed opportunity, and the clever mouse-deer bounded away to safety, leaving the stupid crocodile with the stick in his mouth.

The crocodile, however, determined not to go without his revenge, lay in wait, floating like a water-soaked log until the mouse-deer should visit the river again. When, after a while, he did come to the stream and saw the crocodile motionless, he stood on the bank and said, as if he were in doubt whether or not it was a log, "If that is the crocodile, it will float downstream."

The crocodile, resolving not to give himself away, remained motionless; and then the trickster added, "But if it is a log, it will float upstream." At once the crocodile began to swim slowly against the current, and the mouse-deer, having discovered what he wished, called out in derision, "Ha, ha! I have fooled you once more."

◆

One day a tiger was seeking the mouse-deer to eat him, so the mouse-deer hurried to find a *djati*-plant, whose leaves he chewed making his mouth blood-red, after which he went and sat down beside a well. By and by the tiger came along, and the mouse-deer assumed a fierce aspect, drivelling blood-red saliva from his mouth. "Watch out," he said, "for I am accustomed to eating tigers. If you do not believe it, just look in the well, and you will see the head of the last one that I have finished."

The tiger was much alarmed, though not wholly convinced, so he went to look in the well, where he saw the reflection of his own head. Thinking that this was really the head of the tiger which the mouse-deer had just eaten, and convinced of the mouse-deer's might, the tiger ran away as fast as he could.

Three Fox Stories
Japan

Long, long ago there was an acolyte called Zuiten at a mountain temple. Whenever the priest went away and left Zuiten to take care of the temple alone, a fox would come to the entrance of the priest's living quarters and call, "Zuiten, Zuiten!"

Once it was so provoking that Zuiten went around to the window of the great hall to look out. The fox was standing with his back to the entrance. When he would brush his fat tail on the door, it made a noise, *zui,* and when he would knock his head on the door, it made a sound, *ten.*

Being a clever acolyte, Zuiten quickly went back and stood by the side of the entrance. When he heard *zui,* he yanked the door back, so the fox, who was about to hit his head on the door for *ten,* came tumbling onto the dirt floor of the quarters.

Shutting the door quickly, Zuiten went for a stick and started chasing the fox. While he was running after it, he lost sight of the fox. He went to the great hall to look, and the main image of Buddha seemed to have turned into two images. He could not tell which was the fox in disguise.

"Oh, well, you can't fool me that way," said Zuiten. "The main image at our temple always sticks out his tongue whenever we have services, so I can't make a mistake." Then he began beating the wooden gong and reciting the sutra, and the fox-Buddha hurriedly stuck out a long tongue.

"Now then, I'll serve the food offering to our Buddha over at the quarters," announced Zuiten. "I'll leave the fox behind."

He hurried back to the kitchen and the mock-image came walking brazenly after him.

"First of all, I must give him a bath," said Zuiten, lifting the image into the cauldron over the hearth.

Then Zuiten tied the lid on securely and built up a good fire. By the time the priest returned, the fox was cooked whole and ready for him.

◆

Long, long ago there lived an old man and an old woman in Oshu. The old woman had two eyes, all right, but the old man was one-eyed. Late one day the right-eyed old man changed into a left-eyed old man and came home saying, "Now, Granny, I'm home!"

"This must be a fox," thought the old woman. Aloud she said, "You're home drunk again, aren't you? You always want to get into the straw rice-bag when you come home drunk, you know?"

"Oh, that again!" answered the old man and climbed into the straw bag by himself.

"After you're in the straw bag, you tell me to tie it up on the outside, don't you?" the old woman said.

"Oh, that again?" replied the old man and meekly let her tie him up.

"When I get a rope on this way, you always say to put you on the fire shelf and smoke you, don't you?" said the old woman.

"Oh, that again!" answered the fox again.

Then the old woman swung the fox onto the shelf over the hearth and built a big fire and plagued the fox. She deliberately broiled fish and ate her supper alone, so he could smell the good things. While she was doing this, the real right-eyed old man came home, and the left-eyed one on the shelf was cooked into fox soup.

◆

Long ago a No actor lived in Hiroshima. One day he had gone to a festival at a village by the seashore and was returning alone late at night on the road at the foot of Hijiyama. There was such a cold north wind blowing that he pulled out the mask which he had tucked into his clothes and put it on for a protection against the wind. Then he walked on.

Suddenly a man came down from Hijiyama. "Hello!" he called and stopped the actor. "You're wearing something very unusual on your head. What do you call that thing?" he asked.

"This is a No mask," answered the actor. "This is worn when one does a dance."

"By just wearing that, do you always turn into that face?" asked the stranger. "To tell the truth, I am a fox that lives on Hijiyama. I would like to try disguising myself like you. Please, let me have that thing called a mask."

He begged so earnestly for it that finally the actor agreed. He took off the mask and gave it away and then went home.

Some time after that the feudal lord of Hiroshima set out hunting with a great company of followers. As he led them along the road below Hijiyama, a funny looking fox came out on the mountain. He didn't seem to be the least bit afraid of men, and he made his way down at a leisurely gait.

"Look! A fox has come out," the men all shouted.

A crowd of samurai gathered around and promptly shot it down. Looking closely, they noticed it was wearing the mask of the former No actor. It looked as though he thought that by just putting on the mask, his whole body would turn into the form of a man.

It was said that this fox at Hijiyama was probably the most stupid of all foxes.

The Jelly-fish and the Monkey
Japan

Rin-Jin, the King of the Sea, took to wife a young and beautiful Dragon Princess. They had not been married long when the fair queen fell ill, and all the advice and attention of the great physicians availed nothing.

"Oh," sobbed the queen, "there is only one thing that will cure me of my illness."

"What is that?" inquired Rin-Jin.

"If I eat the liver of a live monkey I shall immediately recover. Pray get me a monkey's liver, for I know that nothing else will save my life."

So Rin-Jin called a jelly-fish to his side, and said, "I want you to swim to the land and return with a live monkey on your back, for I wish to use his liver that our queen may be restored to health again. You are the only creature who can perform this task, for you alone have legs and are able to walk about on shore. In order to induce the monkey to come you must tell him of the wonders of the deep and of the rare beauties of my great palace, with its floor of pearl and its walls of coral."

The jelly-fish, delighted to think that the health and happiness of his mistress depended upon the success of his enterprise, lost no time in swimming to an island. He had no sooner stepped on shore than he observed a fine looking monkey playing about in the branches of a pine tree.

"Hello!" said the jelly-fish, "I don't think much of this island. What a dull and miserable life you must lead here! I come from the Kingdom of the Sea, where Rin-Jin reigns in a palace of great size and beauty. It may be that you would like to see a new country where there is plenty of fruit and where the weather is always fine. If so, get on my back, and

I shall have much pleasure in taking you to the Kingdom of the Sea."

"I shall be delighted to accept your invitation," said the monkey, as he got down from the tree and comfortably seated himself on the thick shell of the jelly-fish.

"By the way," said the jelly-fish, when he had accomplished about half of the return journey, "I suppose you have brought your liver with you, haven't you?"

"What a personal question!" replied the monkey. "Why do you ask?"

"Our Sea Queen is dangerously ill," said the foolish jelly-fish, "and only the liver of a live monkey will save her life. When we reach the palace a doctor will make use of your liver and my mistress will be restored to health again."

"Dear me!" exclaimed the monkey, "I wish you had mentioned this matter to me before we left the island."

"If I had done so," replied the jelly-fish, "you would most certainly have refused my invitation."

"Believe me, you are quite mistaken, my dear jelly-fish. I have several livers hanging up on a pine tree, and I would gladly have spared one in order to save the life of your queen. If you will bring me back to the island again I will get it. It was most unfortunate that I should have forgotten to bring a liver with me."

So the credulous jelly-fish turned round and swam back to the island. Directly the jelly-fish reached the shore the monkey sprang from his back and danced about on the branches of a tree.

"Liver," said the monkey, chuckling, "did you say liver? You silly old jelly-fish, you'll certainly never get mine!"

The jelly-fish at length reached the palace, and told Rin-Jin his dismal tale. The Sea King fell into a great passion. "Beat him to a jelly!" he cried to those about him. "Beat this stupid fellow till he hasn't a bone left in his body!"

So the jelly-fish lost his shell from that unfortunate hour, and all the jelly-fishes that were born in the sea after his death were also without shells, and have remained nothing but jelly to this day.

The Crackling Mountain
Japan

An old man and his wife kept a white hare. One day a badger came and ate the food provided for the pet. The mischievous animal was about to scamper away when the old man, seeing what had taken place, tied the badger to a tree, and then went to a neighboring mountain to cut wood.

When the old man had gone on his journey, the badger began to weep and to beg the old woman to untie the rope. She had no sooner done so than the badger proclaimed vengeance and ran away.

When the good white hare heard what had taken place he set out to warn his master; but during his absence the badger returned, killed the old woman, assumed her form, and converted her corpse into broth.

"I have made such excellent broth," said the badger, when the old man returned from the mountain. "You must be hungry and tired. Pray sit down and make a good meal!"

The old man, not suspecting treachery of any kind, consumed the broth and pronounced it excellent.

"Excellent?" sneered the badger. "You have eaten your wife! Her bones lie over there in that corner." With these words he disappeared.

While the old man was overcome with sorrow, and while

he wept and bewailed his fate, the hare returned, grasped the situation, and scampered off to the mountain fully resolved to avenge the death of his poor old mistress.

When the hare reached the mountain he saw the badger carrying a bundle of sticks on his back. Softly the hare crept up; and, unobserved, set fire to the sticks, which began to crackle immediately.

"This is a strange noise," said the badger. "What is it?"

"The Crackling Mountain," replied the hare.

The fire began to burn the badger, so he sprang into a river and extinguished the flames; but on getting out again he found that his back was severely burnt, and the pain he suffered was increased by a cayenne poultice which the delighted hare provided for that purpose.

When the badger was well again he chanced to see the hare standing by a boat he had made.

"Where are you going in that vessel?" inquired the badger.

"To the moon," replied the hare. "Perhaps you would like to come with me?"

"Not in your boat!" said the badger. "I know too well your tricks on the Crackling Mountain. But I will build a boat of clay for myself, and we will journey to the moon."

Down the river went the wooden boat of the hare and the clay boat of the badger. Presently the badger's vessel began to come to pieces. The hare laughed derisively, and killed his enemy with his oar. Later on, when the loyal animal returned to the old man, he justly received much praise and loving care from his grateful master.

The Miraculous Tea-kettle
Japan

One day a priest of the Morinji *temple put his old tea-kettle* on the fire in order that he might make himself a cup of tea. No sooner had the kettle touched the fire than it suddenly changed into the head, tail, and legs of a badger. The novices of the temple were called in to see the extraordinary sight. While they gazed in utter astonishment, the badger, with the body of a kettle, rushed nimbly about the room, and finally flew into the air. Round and round the room went the merry badger, and the priests, after many efforts, succeeded in capturing the animal and thrusting it into a box.

Shortly after this event had taken place a tinker called at the temple, and the priest thought it would be an excellent idea if he could induce the good man to buy his extraordinary tea-kettle. He therefore took the kettle out of its box, for it had now resumed its ordinary form, and commenced to bargain. The unsuspecting tinker purchased the kettle, and took it away with him, assured that he had done a good day's work in buying such a useful article at so reasonable a price.

That night the tinker was awakened by hearing a curious sound close to his pillow. He looked out from behind his quilts and saw that the kettle he had purchased was not a kettle at all, but a very lively and clever badger.

When the tinker told his friends about his remarkable companion, they said, "You are a fortunate fellow, and we advise you to take this badger on show, for it is clever enough to dance and walk on the tightrope. With song and music you certainly have in this very strange creature a series of novel entertainments which will attract considerable notice, and bring you far more money than you would earn by all the tinkering in the world."

The tinker accordingly acted upon this excellent advice, and the fame of his performing badger spread far and wide. Princes and princesses came to see the show, and from royal patronage and the delight of the common people he amassed a great fortune. When the tinker had made his money he restored the kettle to the *Morinji* temple, where it was worshiped as a precious treasure.

The Turtle and the Monkey
Philippines

Once upon a time there lived a turtle and a monkey in a forest. They were great friends.

Their habitations were separate, but they called on each other on and off. One day when it was the turtle's turn to visit the monkey, he told his friend, "The weather is fine, my dear monkey, let us go out for a walk."

The monkey agreed and they set off on a stroll. They had hardly covered a short distance, when they spotted a young banana plant on one side of the mountain path. The turtle, realizing that the plant could be put to good use, asked the monkey, "What may we do with this nice, green plant?"

The monkey, who presumed himself to be clever, said quickly, "Of course, we will divide the plant. We cut it in two equal parts. I take the upper half, and yours will be the lower."

The plant was accordingly divided. The monkey, thinking that he had a bargain, since the upper part carries the fruit, went away to his home, merrily, with his part. The turtle trudged his slow way, carrying the other part, which was intact with roots. He planted it in his small garden.

The monkey, under the impression that his was the fruit-bearing part, planted it right under the tree on which he and his large family spent most of their time. He kept it under observation, expecting quick results. But the plant wilted and faded away altogether after a few days. It appeared that his dream of enjoying sweet, ripe bananas right in his own little garden was quashed.

The turtle's plant thrived. It grew fast, reaching the fruit-bearing stage in a few weeks. When the bananas ripened, yellow and luscious, the turtle's joy knew no bounds.

The turtle wondered what had happened meanwhile to the monkey's part of the banana plant. He knew that it could not take root. Still, to satisfy his curiosity, he went to call on his friend.

The monkey pulled a long face. "Wherefore are you sad and woebegone?" said the turtle, quite sympathetically.

The monkey replied churlishly, "Don't you see, my plant has died. I am so sad." Then, after a pause, he added, "What about yours?"

Concealing his sense of triumph, the turtle merely observed, "Oh, it is all right. It is already bearing fruit. The bananas are ripe and yellow."

Green with jealousy, and almost stammering, the monkey queried, "That is very interesting. May I see the banana plant?"

"Sure enough, my friend, come along," replied the turtle, unhesitatingly.

Reaching the turtle's home, the monkey saw the banana plant in all its glory—indeed, bent with the weight of bunches of ripened bananas.

Aware that it is not all that easy for the turtle to climb a banana plant, the monkey asked the turtle, "Well, my friend, tell me who is going up to gather the ripe bananas?"

"According to our family tradition, my grandfather will do so," replied the turtle. "He has the skill to climb such sturdy plants."

"So far as I know, your grandfather is now lame," observed the monkey. "I don't think he can scale this tree."

"In that case, I think my brother will climb the plant," said the turtle, carelessly. But he soon knew that he had slipped up, for the monkey laughed and said, "You forgot your brother is blind—completely unfit for a job like this."

Realizing the gravity of the situation, the turtle fell silent. The monkey impishly suggested a way out: "My friend, you let me climb the banana plant. I shall gather the ripened bananas for all of us."

The turtle agreed, since there was no other alternative in sight. The monkey was on top of the banana plant in no time. Snatching one banana after another, he peeled them and ate them, throwing down the peels on all sides. In a few minutes, he nearly gobbled up the whole lot of the ripened fruit.

The turtle was irritated at this unfriendly, selfish behavior of the monkey. He could not stop the plunder of his precious fruit. He shouted, pleadingly, "What are you doing, my friend? You have eaten up my bananas. At least, let me have some."

The monkey, having nearly accomplished his game, would not even reply. He went on eating what was left of the bananas and threw some of the rinds in the direction of the poor turtle.

Insulted at this behavior of the monkey, the turtle decided to teach him a lesson. He collected a stack of thorns from a nearby thicket and put it around the trunk of the banana plant, while the monkey was still munching the last of the bananas.

The turtle respectfully addressed the monkey, "It is no

good your staying put on the banana plant, my friend. I believe you have had your fill. I suggest that you, in your own interest, climb down when you hear the bark of a dog." With that admonition, the turtle left the scene.

A dog barked in the neighborhood. The monkey heard the bark and took notice. He was so much loaded with bananas that he could move with difficulty. Heeding the advice of his friend, the turtle, he commenced to climb down. Heavy in the stomach as he had become, he lost his grip, skidded down, and fell right on the thorns. Scores of thorns pricked his body and he extricated himself from the mesh with great difficulty. His arms, legs, and the rest of his body were painfully bruised; and he reached his place in a pretty bad state, cursing the wily turtle all the time.

Sleep forsook the monkey. He spent most of the night taking out the numerous thorns that had pierced his body. All the time, while forgetting the wrong that he had done to his friend, he contrived means of taking revenge on the turtle.

Getting up early the next morning, he said to himself with grim determination, "I am going to teach the silly turtle a lesson." He left in the direction of the place where the turtle family lived.

Not finding the turtle anywhere and feeling tired, the monkey crouched in the nook of a farm, near a small canal. He actually sat down on a coconut shell. Little did he know that his friend the turtle was inside the shell.

From inside, the turtle pulled hard at the monkey's tail. The monkey was frightened out of his wits and jumped up. He kicked the coconut shell hard and it overturned. There, inside the shell—lo and behold—the monkey found the turtle.

"I have been searching for you everywhere since early morning," shouted the angry monkey. "Then I discover you inside a shell and you have the audacity to twist my tail."

The turtle made no reply. The monkey lifted him up and threatened him, "I must settle my score with you and punish you for your misdeeds."

It was a meek, humbled turtle who said, "After all, you are my friend. What are you going to do with me?"

"I want to roast you alive over red-hot charcoals," screamed the monkey.

The turtle was not taken aback. He merely remarked, without raising his voice, "That's fine. I love red color; that will make me red."

The monkey changed his mind about the punishment, and threatened, "All right, I will cut you to pieces. That is final."

Again, the turtle was not disturbed. His response took the dim-witted monkey by surprise. "That's all right by me. Once you are done with the chopping, you will find a number of turtles crawling around you."

The monkey had a bright idea after all. He shouted in triumph, "I will drop you into the river."

This was indeed the answer to the prayer of the turtle. Smart as he was, he did not show it. Instead he implored the monkey, "My dear friend, please don't do that. I will get drowned. I beseech you, have pity on me! Don't throw me into the river!"

"You are the last creature I would waste my pity on," said the monkey. "How can I forget, or forgive you for the pranks you played at my expense?"

"Please, please, sir," implored the turtle, "burn me over live charcoals or make mincemeat of me. But don't, for God's sake, let me drown in the river. I am afraid of water!"

The monkey heard no more. Lifting the hapless turtle in the air, he dashed him into the river. The poor turtle was lost in an eddy and the monkey thought that was the last of him.

The monkey was about to go back to his home when he

heard a gurgling sound coming from the water. He was amazed to see the turtle showing at the surface, a large fish struggling in the grip of his claws.

"Friend monkey, look here!" shouted the turtle, as if no wrong had been done unto him, "thanks to you, I have caught a big fish."

"Well, well, my friend," remarked the monkey, "give me the fish, or let us share it. I haven't tasted one for a long time."

The turtle knew his opportunity had come at last to even the score for good. He challenged the monkey, "Surely, you can help yourself to catch a bigger fish. Are you that lazy that you want others to feed you all the time?"

The monkey did not relish that expression. To prove that he wasn't lazy, he jumped into the river. Naturally, since he did not know swimming as the turtle did, he drowned. The turtle had the last laugh, as he wended his way home with his catch.

The Mouse Lord Chooses a Bridegroom
Japan

Ages ago, before everything had been decided, the Mouse Lord lived in Japan with his beautiful daughter. When she came of age to be married, he called together all of his advisers to consult with them.

"My daughter," he said, "is far too lovely and noble to marry just anyone. In fact, I have decided to wed her to no one less than the greatest being in the world. Now, who shall it be?"

"The sun," said the first, "is the greatest thing in Japan. Even the Emperor wears the sun as his symbol."

"Why, then, I shall marry her to the sun."

"But," objected the second, stroking his whiskers, "a cloud can cover the sun."

"Obviously, then, she must be married to the cloud."

"But," squeaked the third, "the rain bursts through the clouds and destroys them."

"Surely, then, I must wed her to the rain."

"But," cried the fourth, waving his tail, "no matter how hard the rain falls, it cannot wash away the trees."

"The solution is simple then. She must marry the tree."

"But," peeped the fifth, "a strong wind can blow down the trees."

"Very true. Then the wind must be her husband."

"But," remembered the sixth, scratching his ear, "no matter how hard the wind blows, it cannot blow away the earth."

"Certainly I must marry her to the earth."

"But," observed the seventh, "the earth is buried and imprisoned under the wooden floors of men's houses."

"Without more ado, then, she shall wed the wooden floor."

"But," said the last, his eyes glittering, "however strong the wooden floor, a mouse can gnaw his way through it."

"Doubtless, a mouse must be the greatest being in the world."

And that is how the Mouse Lord's daughter happened to marry a mouse.

The Old Tiger and the Hare
Korea

There was once an old tiger in the hills in Gangwon province. One day he chanced to meet a hare and said, "I am hungry, I am going to eat you up."

The cunning hare answered, "My dear Uncle! Where are you going? I have some delicious food for you. Won't you come with me?"

So the tiger followed the hare into a valley. Then the hare picked up eleven round pebbles and said with a smile, "You have never tasted anything so delicious as this in all your life."

"How do you eat them?" the tiger asked with great interest.

"Oh, it's quite simple," answered the hare. "You just bake them in a fire until they turn red, and then they are most delicious." He lit a fire, and put the pebbles in it.

After a while he said to the tiger, who was gazing hungrily at the fire, "Dear Uncle, I will go and get you some bean sauce. It will make them ever so much better. I'll only be a few minutes. Don't eat them till I get back. There are just ten altogether, for us both, you know."

So the hare ran off and left the tiger alone. While he was waiting the tiger counted the pebbles, which had already turned deep red. He found that there were eleven, not ten, as the hare had said. So he greedily gobbled one of them up, so as to get more than his share. It was so hot that it scorched his tongue, his throat, and his stomach. The pain was unbearable and he rushed madly through the hills in his agony. He had to spend a whole month without eating before he recovered.

One day the tiger met the hare standing by a bush in the

middle of a field. He roared at him angrily, "You tricked me last time. You made me suffer terribly and I have starved for weeks. This time I will certainly eat you up."

The hare trembled with fear but managed to say calmly, "Look here, Uncle. I'm chasing these sparrows now. Don't you see? If you look up at the sky and open your mouth I will drive them into it. You will get thousands of them. Wouldn't that be a much better meal for you than I would make?"

The tiger looked and saw many sparrows fluttering about the bush. He relented somewhat. "You are not trying to trick me again, are you?" he said. "If you mean what you say, I will do as you suggest."

"Oh yes, I mean it all right," replied the hare. "Just stand in the middle of the bush and open your mouth, Uncle."

So the tiger went into the middle of the bush, and looking up at the sky, opened his mouth. Then the hare set fire to the bush. The crackling of the flames sounded like the twittering of a thousand sparrows. The hare shouted, "There's hundreds coming, Uncle. Can't you hear them?" Then he ran away and left the tiger alone in the burning bush. He began to notice that he was getting hot, and then suddenly realized that he was surrounded by fire. It was only with great difficulty that he escaped. All his fur was burnt off, and he could not go out in the cold. He had to stay in his cave for weeks, furious that the hare should have tricked him a second time.

One winter day, when at last his fur had grown again, he went down to a village to look for cattle. He came to a river and there on the bank he met the hare once again. He was furiously angry and roared, "You insignificant wretch! That's twice you have tricked me, and yet you are still alive. What have you got to say for yourself?"

The hare answered most humbly, "Uncle, you don't understand. I've only been trying to help you, but you would not follow my advice. Yet I have come here to get you some fish. The river is full of them, and in winter I live on them. Uncle, have you ever tasted fish? It's the most wonderful thing you ever tasted."

The tiger was curious about fishing, and asked, "How do you catch them? You are not trying to trick me again, are you? This is the last chance I'll give you."

"Do trust me, Uncle," said the hare. "You know the proverb which says, 'Try three times, and you will be successful.' You see those fish down there? Just dip your tail in the water and close your eyes. If you open your eyes, you will scare the fish away. Just keep still, and don't move your tail until I tell you. It makes a fine fishing rod!"

The tiger saw the fish in the river, and so he dipped his tail in the cold water. He stood there patiently with his eyes closed. The hare waded up and down in the river and shouted to the tiger, "I'm chasing the fish over to your tail. The water is very cold, but keep still just the same. Your tail will soon feel very heavy."

It was now evening. It was very cold indeed and the water in the river began to freeze. Soon the tiger's tail was frozen fast. The hare shouted, "Uncle! I think you should have caught quite a lot by now. Just lift your tail, and you will see." The tiger tried and found that his tail was very heavy indeed. With a happy smile he said, "I must have caught a lot. It's so heavy I can't move it."

Then the hare shouted as he ran off, "Uncle Tiger! You have tried to kill me, but you are caught now, and you will never get away."

Then the tiger realized that his tail was frozen firmly in the ice, and so he could not go back to the mountains. In the morning the villagers found the tiger still squatting on the ice and a hunter caught it without the slightest difficulty.

The Locust, the Ant, and the Kingfisher
Korea

Once upon a time a locust, an ant, and a kingfisher decided to hold a party. The locust and the kingfisher were to go and get the fish, and the ant was to prepare the rice. So they went off separately to find the various foods.

The ant met a peasant woman who was carrying a basket of rice on her head. It crawled up her leg and bit her, so that she jumped and the basket of rice fell off her head. Then the ant snatched it up and carried it off.

The locust went down to the lake and sat on a leaf that was floating on the water. A fish came and swallowed it, and then the kingfisher, which had been waiting nearby, swooped down and caught the fish, and took it to the party.

The locust came out of the fish, and began to quarrel with the kingfisher over who had caught it. He insisted that he had caught it, while the kingfisher insisted that he had.

The ant burst out laughing when he saw them quarreling. He laughed so much that his waist became thin, just as it is today. The locust took hold of the kingfisher by his bill and pulled, so that it became the long bill we see now. And the kingfisher bit the locust's head, so that it got its present shape.

Myths
and Legends

Stories about cultural heroes and heroines help people to understand their past, real or imagined. They bind a group together by providing a common history which distinguishes them from their neighbors. The question of whether people generally believe these stories to be true—a qualification which is sometimes part of the definition of the terms *myth* and *legend*—is difficult to answer, and may well be irrelevant in the case of these stories. If "true" means literally factual in every detail, then probably few people have ever believed any of these stories to be true. If it means that they contain abstract or metaphorical truths, or commonly held images of the culture's heroes, then most people in a given culture probably do accept them on these terms.

The first two stories in this section, "Archer Hou Yi and Chang-O" and "The Herdsboy and the Weaving Maid" are ancient Chinese stories which have become part of the native lore of Korea, Japan, and Vietnam as well, and help to define the broadly based East Asian cultural region.

The following three stories from Japan, "The Sea Palace," "Momotaro, the Peach Boy," and "Kaguya Himé," tell of supernatural men and women whose fictional deeds have left their imprint on Japanese culture. And finally, "The Ballad of Mulan," "The Supernatural Crossbow," and "Rajah Soliman's Daughter" are stories about historical people whose tragic or heroic lives have become immortalized in popular narratives. Supernatural events blend with realistic details in "The Supernatural Crossbow," while the stories of Mulan and Rajah Soliman's Daughter approach romanticized history.

Archer Hou Yi and Chang-O
China

In ancient times there were ten brother suns whose task it was to give light and warmth to the earth. Every day one brother in turn made his journey across the sky, while the other nine suns rested in the Fusang Tree to the east. But after some time the brothers got tired of waiting nine days each for his own turn, and decided to go out all at once. The appearance of ten suns brought severe drought to the earth. The fields were parched so that no plants could grow, the streams and ponds dried up so that there was no water to drink, trees withered, the earth cracked, and it seemed that the very stones would melt under the suns' intense heat.

The Heavenly Emperor Di Jun, father of the ten suns, saw how the people on earth were suffering. Saddened that so many people had already died from the severe heat, and that many who survived were nothing but blackened skin and bones, he sent the Archer Hou Yi from heaven to frighten the suns into returning to their proper order.

Hou Yi took the red bow and ten white arrows which Di Jun had given him, fitted one arrow to his bow, and shot in the direction of the suns. Suddenly a great fireball fell, surrounded by a cloud of black feathers. A large black lump landed on the earth, which on closer inspection turned out to be a three-legged crow, the transformed body of one of the suns. Hou Yi shot again and again, each time hitting another of the suns; and each time a three-legged crow fell to the ground. In his anger at the suffering caused by the suns' willful behavior, Hou Yi wanted to shoot them all, but the wise Earthly Emperor Yao stole the tenth arrow from his quiver, so that one sun remained in the sky.

Hou Yi had accomplished the task the Heavenly Emperor Di Jun had set for him, but in doing so had killed nine of the Emperor's sons. In punishment for this Di Jun did not allow him to return to Heaven, but banished him to the world of mortals.

Hou Yi had a beautiful wife named Chang-O who had accompanied him to earth. When she learned that they both had been banished from Heaven she was exceedingly angry, and constantly berated her husband and nagged him to find a way for them to return.

Chang-O had heard of a goddess named Queen Mother of the West who lived in the Kunlun Mountains and was reported to have an elixir of immortality. She begged her husband to go and get some of the elixir, in the hope that even if they could not return to Heaven, at least they could be immortals here on earth. With great difficulty Hou Yi sought out the Queen Mother of the West. Crossing the Fiery Peaks of constantly erupting volcanoes and the Moat of Weak Water on which not even a feather will float, at last he reached the Queen Mother's home in the Kunlun Mountains.

Touched by Hou Yi's story and impressed by his brave deeds, the Queen Mother of the West agreed to give him the last of her elixir of immortality. She cautioned him that it was only enough to let one person ascend to Heaven as a deity, but it was sufficient to let two people become earthly immortals.

When Hou Yi returned and told Chang-O about the elixir she was exceedingly happy. At first she agreed that they would share the elixir and stay together as immortals on earth. But the more she thought about the joys of her previous life in Heaven, the more she longed to return there. So while her husband was resting from his long journey she opened the bag of elixir and ate it all herself.

Gradually her body became lighter, her feet left the floor, and she began to float into the air and out the window. Higher and higher she floated, until she found herself on the cold, silvery moon. Alas! She was indeed a heavenly goddess once again, but because of her selfish deed she was confined to a cold and lonely place with nothing but a rabbit, a toad, and a cassia tree to keep her company.

The Herdsboy and the Weaving Maid
China

Long ago there was a young boy who lived with his older brother and his brother's wife. The couple cared little for the boy and did not even give him a name, but since he spent most of his time in the fields tending water buffalo everyone called him the Herdsboy. When the Herdsboy was old enough to care for himself, his elder brother divided the family property, keeping the fields and farmhouse for himself, giving the Herdsboy only the water buffalo, and sending him away to make his own living.

The Herdsboy led the buffalo to the greenest pastures to feed, and took it to the freshest streams to drink. He built a straw hut for himself and a shed for the buffalo, and made a meager living plowing the villagers' rice fields. He loved his buffalo and took tender care of it, but still he was lonely for human companionship and longed to have a wife.

One day the buffalo said to the Herdsboy, "Tomorrow evening, climb over the hill, and there you will see some fairy maidens bathing in a pool. They will leave their clothing on the grass, and you must go and take the the pink gauze robe. The maiden who comes looking for her robe will become your wife."

The next day the Herdsboy did as the buffalo had said. In the evening he climbed the hill and then descended to the pool at the foot of the hill. Hiding behind some shrubbery nearby, he watched as several fairy maidens splashed and played in the water. Seeing that they were completely absorbed in their games, he crept out and gathered up the pink gauze robe that was lying on the grass, then once again hid behind the shrubbery. Soon the fairy maidens came out of the water and began to comb their hair and put on their robes. One of them could not find her robe and began looking everywhere for it.

Venturing farther and farther from the pool she looked in the nearby woods. There she encountered the Herdsboy, who gave her back her robe. Entranced by her beauty, he asked her her name and where she came from.

"I am the granddaughter of the Queen Mother of the Western Heaven," she replied. "I am called Weaving Maid, because I weave brocade with which my grandmother decorates the sky. Day and night I work at my loom making rose-colored brocade, but I never see the sunrise and sunset into which it is made. Though I live in heaven, it is like a prison. My friends and I have long wished to escape if only for a moment, to visit the world of mortals and see how mortals live. Today my grandmother drank a bit too much wine and dozed off for a moment, and we took this chance to visit the mortal world. But now I fear my friends have gone back without me. What am I to do?"

"Stay here with me," said the Herdsboy.

The Herdsboy and the Weaving Maid loved each other very much, and they set up a household together, the Herdsboy farming the fields with his faithful buffalo, and the Weaving Maid weaving in their little thatched cottage. Soon the Weaving Maid gave birth to a son, and then to a daughter.

But the Queen Mother of the Western Heaven was angry at the Weaving Maid's absence, and when, after many months of searching, she discovered that her granddaughter had taken up with a mortal in the land below she could not contain her anger. Enraged, she descended to earth and dragged the Weaving Maid back with her to heaven.

No matter how the Herdsboy and the Weaving Maid wept and pleaded, the Queen Mother would not relent. Heartbroken from their separation, the Herdsboy could not work and the Weaving Maid would not weave. In exasperation, the Queen Mother turned them both into stars and set them on either side of the River of Heaven, the Milky Way.

The Weaving Maid is the star Vega, and the Herdsboy is Altair; the two lesser stars near Altair are their two children, whom he kept at his side as he searched for his wife, their mother. All year long the Herdsboy and the Weaving Maid are separated from each other by the Milky Way, and especially in the summer months their tears fall to earth as heavy rain.

The creatures on earth feel great pity for their suffering, and every year, on the seventh day of the seventh month of the lunar year, all the magpies on earth fly to heaven to form a bridge over the Milky Way. On that night the two lovers meet on the Magpie Bridge for one night of joyful reunion.

The Sea Palace
Japan

The god Ninigi had three sons, of whom the eldest was Hoderi no Mikoto and the youngest Hoori no Mikoto. Hoderi no Mikoto was very fond of sea-fishing and was in charge of the marine products, while his younger brother Hoori no Mikoto was wonderfully clever at hunting and was in charge of all game. One day Hoori no Mikoto proposed to his brother, saying, "Dear brother, what do you say to our changing places? I want to go fishing today." At first Hoderi no Mikoto flatly spurned the proposal, but moved by his brother's earnest and repeated entreaties he at last agreed, though not with very good grace, and lent him his fishing tackle.

As an angler, however, Hoori no Mikoto proved a complete failure; he had no success whatever, and, what was worse, by some accident he lost the hook he had borrowed from his brother. Hoderi no Mikoto was greatly annoyed at the loss of his hook, and insisted so persistently upon getting it back at once that Hoori no Mikoto melted his sword into five hundred hooks. These he offered to his brother by way of compensation, but they were rejected. Then he made a thousand hooks of fine quality in the same way and took them to his brother. Hoderi refused to accept them too, saying that he did not want any hook except the one that he had lent.

One day, at a loss what to do, Hoori stood weeping by the seashore, when the god Shiotsuchi happened to pass by, and, after listening to Hoori's account, felt sorry for him in his predicament, and said, "I have a good idea to help you out of your trouble and make you happy." And he hurriedly built a small boat which was perfectly watertight, put Hoori aboard, and floated it out onto the sea.

When he had sailed out for some time he found himself in front of the beautiful palace where dwelt Watatsu no Kami, the Sea God. By the entrance gate was a well over which spread the branches of a Japanese Judas tree with a fragrant perfume. Hoori climbed up the tree and surveyed the inside of the palace. Presently the maid waiting on Toyotama Himé, the daughter of the Sea God, came out carrying a beautiful jar to draw water from the well. She was very much surprised to see the figure of a man reflected in the water, and even more surprised when she looked up and perceived a noble-looking youth sitting on a branch of the tree.

Hoori asked the maid for some water; she drew some water in the jar and held it out to the stranger. Instead of drinking it, he took a jewel off his necklace, put it into his mouth, and then spat it out into the jar. The jewel stuck fast to the jar, and try as she might, the maid could not remove it, so she was obliged to take the jar, just as it was, to Toyotama Himé, telling her about the handsome stranger and what he had done.

When the Sea God heard of the young man he came out to see who he was. Knowing at a glance that he was the son of the god Ninigi, he respectfully invited him into the palace and offered his daughter's hand in marriage. That night a grand banquet was given in celebration of the

Princess's wedding to Hoori no Mikoto, and the newly-wedded couple lived happily together in the palace for the next three years.

One night something reminded Hoori of his dear old home, and he heaved a deep sigh of bitter grief. This caused a great deal of concern to his wife who was sitting by his side. She secretly sent word to her father saying, "My husband has lived here with me these three years very happily and without the slightest show of worry of grief, but tonight I heard him heave a long and deep sigh. What can be the matter with him? It worries me."

The Sea God, who was as concerned as his daughter, went to his son-in-law, and inquired into the cause of this grief. Thereupon Hoori no Mikoto told him all that had passed between his brother and himself.

Watatsu no Kami summoned into his presence all the fishes, large and small, and asked if one among them had swallowed the hook Hoori had lost. Then a sea bream complained that he could not eat anything, having something stuck in his throat. The Sea God at once ordered it to be pulled out, and washing it in clean water, submitted it to the inspection of Hoori, who with extreme joy recognized it as the very hook he had borrowed from his brother.

Then the Sea God gave his son-in-law the following suggestion, "When you return the hook to your brother, you must be careful to hand it to him while standing with your back to him and uttering the incantation, 'This is *Obochi*, this is *Susuchi*, this is *Majichi*, this is *Uruchi*.' And, if your brother cultivates a high rice field, you are advised to cultivate a low one; if he cultivates a low rice field, you had better try a high one. I will so arrange that your rice fields shall be better irrigated. After the lapse of three years you will surely become very rich and prosperous, and with your brother it will fare worse and worse."

So saying, he took out two beads and added, "And, if he

feels bitter against you and comes to hurt you, take out this 'Flood-causing Bead'; it will drown him. If he surrenders, take out this 'Ebb-inducing Bead'; it will prevent him from drowning."

Then he called the sharks together and said, "Now, the son of the Heavenly God is leaving for home. How quickly can any one of you carry him home and get back?" One of them answered, "I will do that in a day." The Sea God placed Hoori on the shark's neck and sent them away, cautioning the carrier not to give the rider the slightest cause for fear during the journey.

Hoori arrived on the shore safe and sound, and when the shark was going back he took off his short sword and tied it around its neck. Hoori no Mikoto restored the hook to his brother exactly the way the Sea God had instructed. His subsequent life was an unbroken flow of good fortune and happiness, but the reverse was the case with his brother Hoderi no Mikoto. He vented his vexation in persecuting Hoori. But Hoori followed the suggestions of the Sea God and succeeded at last in bringing Hoderi to his knees. Thereafter Hoderi no Mikoto remained in the service of Hoori no Mikoto, tending over him day and night.

Momotaro, the Peach Boy
Japan

Since the beginning of time, everyone in Japan has loved children. Nor did anyone ever love them more than the old woodcutter and his wife, who lived on the edge of the forest in a distant province. So it was no wonder that, as the years went by and they had no child, they grew sadder and sadder. Still they went about their business cheerfully, and continued to offer prayers and sacrifices to the gods in hope that their wish might be fulfilled.

One day the woodcutter went off to the forest and his wife went down to the stream to do some washing. As she knelt over the water, she noticed a large peach bobbing on the surface. It was the biggest, most beautiful golden peach she had ever seen. Quickly she reached out and grabbed it, and carried it joyfully home.

When the old man returned home that evening, his wife cried out, "See what a lovely thing I have for you?" The old man had never seen such a splendid piece of fruit, and he hardly dared cut it open. Just as he touched the knife to its skin, the peach burst open of its own accord. Inside was a beautiful little baby boy, laughing happily. His skin was as warm and golden, soft and blushing as that of the peach, and his nature seemed even sweeter. The old man and woman stepped back in surprise.

"Surely the gods have answered our prayers," said the old woman, "and given us a son in our old age."

"Indeed," replied the woodcutter. "So we shall call him Momotaro, the son of the peach, in their honor."

The woodcutter and his wife took loving care of Momotaro and every day were more richly rewarded. For every day Momotaro grew more handsome and wise, sweeter and stronger. One day he came and knelt before them.

"Grandfather and grandmother," he said, "you have ever been kind and good to me, and there is none I love more in the world. But now I must leave you for a while. For I am a man now, and must go out to prove myself and help others."

The old woman grew fearful. "But where will you go?" she cried.

"I must go far beyond the village," replied Momotaro,

"to the Oni Island. There I shall conquer the *oni* and bring back the treasure they have stolen. Therefore I beg you to make for me some dumplings, for it will be a long journey."

Now the *oni* are horrible ogres, huge as pine trees, with horns like a demon's and tusks like those of an elephant. Their bodies are red and blue and green, and sometimes even black as their deeds. For many ages they had laid waste the countryside, killing everyone in their path and stealing Japan's most priceless treasures. So no one could blame the old woman for trembling and begging Momotaro not to go. But Momotaro reassured her and promised that he would soon come home to them.

The old woman went off and made some dumplings, as her son had asked. Meanwhile, the woodcutter gave Momotaro a new pair of trousers, a sharp sword, and a little flag on which was written, "Japan's Number-One Momotaro." With many sighs, they bade each other farewell.

But as Momotaro left the village, his heart grew lighter and his step quicker, as he thought of the adventures ahead. He walked down a deserted road and heard a rustling in the bushes. A great dog jumped out.

"I am Lord Dog," he growled, "Who trespasses on my land?"

"Japan's Number-One Momotaro," replied the peach boy.

The dog bowed low. "Ah, Momotaro, we have heard of you. Please accept my humble services as your retainer."

"Certainly," said Momotaro, giving the dog a dumpling. "Now eat this, and you will have the strength of ten men."

Momotaro and Lord Dog walked on a bit further. Soon they heard a chattering in the treetops, and a slender monkey swung down.

"I am Lord Monkey," he shrieked. "Who trespasses on my land?"

"Japan's Number-One Momotaro."

The monkey bowed low. "Ah, Momotaro, we have heard of you. Please accept my humble services as your retainer."

"Certainly," said Momotaro, giving the monkey a dumpling.

The three went on together until late afternoon. Suddenly they heard a great whirring in the air. A splendid pheasant flew down before them.

"I am Lord Pheasant," he sang. "Who trespasses on my land?"

"Japan's Number-One Momotaro."

The pheasant bowed low. "Ah, Momotaro, we have heard of you. Please accept my humble services as your retainer."

"Certainly," said Momotaro, giving the pheasant a dumpling.

So on they traveled, until they reached the sea. They found a small boat, and rowed and rowed across the deep, dark waters. Finally, at nightfall they reached the gates of the Oni Castle. The castle was gloomy and gray, and a huge black cloud hung over it like a bad omen. From inside came the sounds of a wild feast. For a moment they grew afraid. But by that time they had eaten all the dumplings; they had the strength of thousands of men.

"Now," declared Momotaro, "is the time to strike."

Up climbed the monkey to the top of the wall, while the pheasant flew to the gatepost, and the dog hid behind the gate. Momotaro banged loudly on the gate. Out came an ugly red *oni*, in an even worse temper than usual at having been disturbed.

"Who are you, silly little insect, making so much noise?"

"Japan's Number-One Momotaro, come to conquer you."

The *oni* laughed horribly, looking like a bad dream. He lumbered back to the castle to tell the others the joke. Soon hordes of *oni* came swarming out to see the funny human bug who thought he could conquer them. But as they came through the gates, the pheasant flew down and pecked out their eyes. The monkey swung by his tail and twisted their necks. The dog leapt upon them and knocked them down, while Momotaro finished them off with his sword. When three thousand *oni* had been killed, the rest drew back and bowed in surrender.

"Oh, mighty Momotaro," wept their leader, "please forgive us. We see now that we are no match for you."

"I shall forgive you," replied Momotaro, "only if you promise to give back all the treasure you have stolen, and never to do evil again."

The *oni* gave their promise, and hurried to unlock the treasure house. Momotaro, Lord Dog, Lord Monkey, and Lord Pheasant wheeled the treasure back in a huge cart, and restored it to its rightful owners. When the Emperor heard of their noble deeds, he granted them a rich reward and declared a day of thanksgiving. Momotaro returned to the overjoyed woodcutter and his wife, bringing with him his three faithful retainers. They lived together in comfort and happiness for many years, and Japan was never troubled by the *oni* again.

Kaguya Himé
Japan

Far back in the history of Japan there lived in a village near Kyoto a peasant couple. The name of the husband was Sanuki no Miyatsuko Maro, but he was generally known as Taketori, or Bamboo Cutter.

Every day he made his way up the mountain slopes to cut

bamboo canes, out of which he made various articles, selling them in the market to gain a scanty living. Though they had little they were well contented with their lot. They calmly took what Heaven sent—the bitter and the sweet, the smooth and the rough—and lived a life as happy and free as any simple-hearted married couple. But one thing and one thing only was wanting to complete their happiness: They lacked a child to fill their hearts with joy and their home with light.

One day while cutting bamboo on the hill as usual, the old man noticed that a soft, ethereal radiance streamed out from the lower section of the bamboo. His curiosity was whetted. He drew near to the bamboo, and with the greatest care possible, cut it, when a strange sight broke upon his gaze. From out of the cane there burst forth a tiny babe, no larger than his middle finger, a charming girl smiling a radiant, angelic smile.

For a moment Taketori could not believe his eyes, but when he had gathered his scattered wits he felt sure that the gods had at last answered his prayer. He thanked the gods, and with a heart full of gladness, ran homeward, cherishing the treasure in his hand.

When he reached home his head was in a whirl. He wanted to speak, but his lips refused to obey him. Presently, however, he related to his astonished wife what had happened. She would not have believed his words had she not seen the child herself. They brought up the child as the apple of their eyes.

Months grew into years as their child grew into budding womanhood. Her face was beautiful beyond compare; her hair was raven black; her skin delicate as a cherry blossom; and her smile perfectly angelic. Besides, wherever she was, awake or asleep, the halo of a mysterious radiance encircled her person; so they called her "Kaguya Himé," or the Illumined Princess.

Her fame spread far and wide under the sun, from Taro to Jiro, from Jiro to Tagosaku, and many a gallant of the village sought her hand, daily flocking to the door of the old couple's cottage. But Kaguya Himé never emerged from the parental roof, nor did she admit any stranger inside. Most of them came at length to regard her as an unobtainable angel, and gave up their visits in despair.

Five youths, however, remained undismayed. Zealously, they besieged her with letters penned with all the fire of passion, and though they were not encouraged by a reply, they continued to pour forth their love. Finally the maiden, affected by the ardor of their devotion, granted them an audience in which she demanded that they each should accomplish a certain task before they could win her hand.

Of the first suitor she requested the Buddha's Rice Bowl; of the second the Skin of a Fire-rat; of the third the Jewel from the neck of a Dragon; of the fourth the Golden Bough which flourished on Mount Horai; of the fifth the Koya-sugai, a shell of talismanic virtue. Then the young competitors, without a moment's delay, set out on their respective missions—each in a different direction—missions on which their fortunes hung. But alas! All their efforts came to naught and their burning desire still remained ungratified.

The tidings of this lovely maiden spread further to the court, reaching the august ears of the Emperor. His Majesty sent a messenger to her twice, bidding her appear in the court, but she gave him the same answer as she did to her many adorers.

Three years had now elapsed, when a sudden change came over the maiden. On every moonlit night, from the beginning of spring, she would look up into the boundless heavens with a faraway look, and then would fall to sobbing. From her strange mien one could derive no ray of comfort or hope; about her lips there played no smile; only sorrow and worry could one perceive on her lovely face.

This caused her gray-haired parents great anxiety. They took their meals but the food would not go down their throats. They worked in the fields and mountains but not the slightest happiness would come out of their work. They slept, but their sleep was marred by nightmares. Their home was dark and dismal. At last in their anxiety, they asked her why she grieved so. To this Kaguya Himé gave the following answer:

"Many a time have I intended to open my heart to you, but fearing it might give you grief, I dared not do so till this moment. The time has come for me at last to reveal all my secrets to you. To tell the truth, I am a native of Moon Land, but owing to some unavoidable circumstances I have been obliged to dwell down here in this world. Now, on the fifteenth of the eighth month, when the moon is full, a messenger will come down from Heaven to take me up there. And oh!" here her voice trembled, "Oh! my heart nearly breaks as I think of bidding eternal farewell to this village where, amidst comfort and enjoyment, my childhood was passed." She burst forth with loud sobbing into a flood of tears as she spoke these last words.

How terribly shocked the old couple were at this marvelous revelation! They declared that Kaguya Himé, whom they had brought up from her infancy, could never be a child born in Moon Land, and indignantly said that she should not be taken away from them even for a moment.

But should she continue her existence in this world, heavenly punishment would descend upon her; and should she set out on her aerial journey to the Moon, how sorely the aged man and wife would miss her! She was in a perfect dilemma, from which she could by no means escape but by sacrificing one of her desires. She had no choice but to sacrifice the future happiness of the old couple for the sake of the celestial commandment.

So she addressed her parents: "It is really against my will

that I leave this hamlet for the Upper World. Pray, therefore, put yourselves in my place in this predicament and do not take it amiss."

The news reached the Emperor, who, wishing for the particulars of the matter, sent a messenger to the cottage. To this messenger the old man, half in sobs, related that their daughter was inclined to return to Moon Land on the fifteenth of the eighth month, and that his grief had made his hair as white as snow. When the Emperor heard the whole story, he felt very compassionate toward the poor old bamboo cutter and promised to send a large force of soldiers that day to guard Kaguya Himé against the visit of the Moon Land men.

Now when the fifteenth day came the Emperor dispatched, as he had promised, an army of two thousand soldiers with a lieutenant-general in command. The soldiers were armed with bows and arrows, some standing on the hills hard by, others on the roofs. The old woman sat in a lacquered palanquin in the main house with Kaguya Himé in her arms. As for the old man, he donned his armor and helmet and stood beside the palanquin, which was tightly closed. Old as he was, he was prepared for the worst.

The night had far advanced and midnight approached, when the surroundings of the house suddenly brightened up. A great multitude of heavenly beings, adorned with jewels and diamonds, descended on many-colored clouds, carrying a flying couch; they formed a long line, keeping a distance of five feet from the earth. The armed guards, both inside and out, tried to release their arrows against them, but, strange to say, their limbs instantly became cramped and they could not stir a finger.

Meanwhile, one of the celestial beings imperiously summoned the old man and addressed him thus:

"Listen to me, old man. I am the King of Moon Land. Kaguya Himé, whom you cherish as the apple of your eye, is not a creature of the earth but of the skies. She committed a sin for which she was expelled from the heavens and was doomed to live with you for a while. But the time has come to a close and we are come to receive her. So you should not be reluctant to give her back to us."

Amazed and bewildered, Taketori did not know what to do. All that he could do was to prostrate himself at a respectful distance from the heavenly emissary and mutter. After a while, however, he composed himself and said to the King, "May it please Your Majesty, the Kaguya Himé whom you have come to summon must be another maiden of the same name. Our Kaguya Himé has lived with us for some twenty years and not for 'a while,' as you say. And if she be the very maiden whom you are in quest of, she should not be allowed to depart from hence, for she has been affected with a serious disease during the past few weeks."

But the King, ignoring what he said, had the couch brought upon the roof. "Come forth, Kaguya," shouted the King. The door of the palanquin opened of itself, and out came the maiden. She drew near the weeping couple.

"'Tis a thousand pities," she said, "that I take leave of you without returning the many favors you have heaped upon me. But it cannot be helped, for anything and everything depends entirely upon the King's will, and not upon my own. May the remainder of your lives be happy and prosperous."

But the old man and woman only cried imploringly, "How can you go, our dearest, leaving behind you these two withered figures whom only death awaits? If you must go, why would you not take us with you?" They were nearly beside themselves in the agony of their grief.

At this tragic juncture Kaguya Himé took off one of her garments, which she handed to Taketori along with a letter, saying, "This garment I leave with you as a keepsake. You may regard it just as myself and whenever your heart aches for me, look at it. Thus you can to some extent console yourself."

Scarcely had she finished these last words when one of the Moon Land people took out the Elixir of Immortality and offered it to the maiden. After tasting some of it she wished to present the remainder to Taketori, but they forbade her to do so. Just then a *hagoromo* [robe of feathers] was brought before her which she was to wear, but she begged them to wait for a while, for she had something more to do.

She wrote another letter addressed to the Emperor and handed it to his messenger along with the Elixir of Immortality. Then she put on the *hagoromo,* boarded the couch, and started on her aerial journey to the heavenly capital, rigorously defended by numberless guardian angels.

The eyes of all those assembled followed the couch intently. It went up and up until it was a mere speck in the skies, and then was lost to sight. With the disappearance of the couch the mantle of darkness again fell over the house, and the elderly couple were found mourning more grievously than ever.

The lieutenant-general, commander of the army, began to read the letter which the maiden had left behind for the two, but they would not listen to him. He held forth the Elixir of Immortality this time, but they would not even touch it. They did nothing but weep and wail until bloodlike tears rolled down their cheeks in torrents. Every resource to soothe them exhausted, the commander and his soldiers quitted the spot, though they were loath to part from the heartbroken couple.

When the Emperor heard of all that had happened, he was disheartened beyond measure. He called his chamberlain and inquired if he happened to know which mountain rose nearest to the skies. The chamberlain replied that in the province of Suruga there towered Japan's loftiest mountain. Thereupon His Majesty sent his messenger to the mountain with the Elixir of Immortality to burn it on its summit. It is said the smoke has never died away, even after hundreds of years. From that time down to the present, Mount Fuji has been called the Mountain of Immortality.

The Ballad of Mulan
China

Mulan's swift fingers flying to and fro
Crossed warp with woof in deft and even row,
As by the side of spinning-wheel and loom
She sat at work without the women's room.
But tho' her hand the shuttle swiftly plies
The whir cannot be heard for Mulan's sighs;
When neighbor asked what ills such mood had
    wrought,
And why she worked in all-absorbing thought,
She answered not, for in her ears did ring
The summons of last evening from the King,
Calling to arms more warriors for the west,
The name of Mulan's father heading all the rest.
But he was ill—no son to take his place;
Excuses meant suspicion and disgrace.
Her father's honor must not be in doubt;
Nor friends, nor foe, his stainless name shall flout.
She would herself his duty undertake
And fight the Northern foe for honor's sake.

Her purpose fixed, the plan was soon evolved,
But none should know it, this she was resolved;

Alone, unknown, she would the danger face,
Relying on the prowess of her race.
A charger here, a saddle there, she bought,
And next a bridle and a whip she sought;
With these equipped she donned the soldier's gear,
Arming herself with bow and glittering spear.
And then before the sun began his journey steep
She kissed her parents in their troubled sleep,
Caressing them with fingers soft and light,
She quietly passed from their unconscious sight;
And mounting horse, she with her comrades rode
Into the night to meet what fate forbode.
And as her secret not a comrade knew,
Her fears soon vanished as the morning dew.

That day they galloped westward fast and far,
Nor paused until they saw the evening star;
Then by the Yellow River's rushing flood
They stopped to rest and cool their fevered blood.
The turbid stream swept on with swirl and foam
Dispelling Mulan's dreams of friends and home.
Mulan! Mulan! she heard her mother cry—
The waters roared and thundered in reply!
Mulan! Mulan! she heard her father sigh—
The river surged in angry billows by!
The second night they reach the River Black,
And on the range which feeds it, bivouac;
Mulan! Mulan! she hears her father pray—
While on the ridge the Tartars' horses neigh.
Mulan! Mulan! her mother's lips let fall—
The Tartars' camp sends forth a bugle call!

The morning dawns on men in armed array
Aware that death may meet them on that day;
The winter sun sends forth a pallid light

Through frosty air on knights in armor bright;
While bows strung taut, and spears in glittering rows
Forebode the struggle of contending foes.
And soon the trumpets blare—the fight's begun;
A deadly melee, and the Pass is won!
The war went on, and many a battle-field
Revealed Mulan both bow and spear could wield;
Her skill and courage won her widespread fame,
And comrades praised, and leaders of great name.

Then after several years of march and strife,
Mulan and others, who had 'scaped with life
From fields of victory drenched with patriots' blood
Returned again to see the land they loved.
And when at last the Capital was reached,
The warriors, who so many forts had breached,
Were summoned to the presence of the King,
And courtiers many did their praises sing.
Money and presents on them, too, were showered,
And some with rank and office were empowered,
While Mulan, singled out from all the rest,
Was offered fief and guerdon of the best.
But gifts and honors she would gladly lose
If she might only be allowed to choose
Some courier camels, strong and fleet of pace,
To bear her swiftly to her native place.

And now, at last, the journey nears the end,
and father's, mother's voices quickly blend,
In "Mulan, Mulan! Welcome, welcome, dear!"
And this time there was naught but joy to fear.
Her younger sisters decked the house with flowers,
And loving words fell sweet as summer showers;
Her little brother shouted Mulan's praise,
For many proud and happy boastful days!

The greetings o'er, she slipped into her room,
Radiant with country flowers in fragrant bloom,
And changed her soldier's garb for woman's dress:
Her head adorned with simple maiden's tress,
A single flower enriched her lustrous hair,
And forth she came, fresh, maidenly, and fair!
Some comrades in the war had now come in,
Who durst not mingle in the happy din;
But there in awe and admiration stood,
As brave men do before true womanhood.
For not the boldest there had ever dreamed,
On toilsome march, or when swords flashed and
gleamed
In marshalled battle, or on sudden raid,
That their brave comrade was a beauteous maid.

The Supernatural Crossbow
Vietnam

More than two thousand and three hundred years ago, the story goes, a king of the land of the Thuc asked for the hand of a princess of the house of Hong Bang, which ruled over the realm of Van Lang, as Vietnam was then called. The marriage proposal was met with an abrupt refusal, so embittering the king that he vowed to bring about the downfall of the Hong Bang. But he died without having succeeded in carrying out his vow of hatred, thus willing the task as a legacy to his heirs. This was the origin of a protracted state of warfare between the kingdoms of Thuc and Van Lang.

For a number of years the Hong Bang emerged always victorious from the feuding. Finally, heartened by an unbroken string of military successes and confident of the protection of the divine spirits, the Hong Bang gradually relaxed their vigilance and lulled themselves into idleness and the pursuit of pleasure.

Meantime their enemy, in the person of King Thuc Phan, was undertaking extensive and meticulous preparations, and awaiting a propitious moment for the invasion of Van Lang. When the time was ripe, he crushed the army of the eighteenth Hong Bang king.

When he realized that his cause was lost, the king of Van Lang became fearfully angry. The blood vessels in his throat burst, his blood flowed in streams from his mouth, and he ran and flung himself down a deep well. Thus ended the life of the last king of a dynasty which had descended from Than Nong, one of the five great emperors of ancient China, a legendary dynasty that is said to have lasted for perhaps more than two thousand and six hundred years.

Thuc Phan reunited the two kingdoms under the name of Au Lac, and he himself took the name and title of An Duong Vuong or King An Duong. He established his capital in the territory of Phong Khe. But scarcely were the ramparts erected than a violent storm broke in the night, and they collapsed. Three times more did An Duong have the embankments reconstructed; three times more were they destroyed in a single night.

So the king then caused an altar to be erected beyond the eastern gate, and there he began to pray to the gods. On the seventh day of the third month he saw coming from the east an old man, who said to him, "You can count upon the cooperation of the ambassador of the Limpid Waters."

Next day, very early in the morning, the king noticed an enormous golden tortoise which came from the east, moving swiftly over the surface of the water. Speaking the language of men, this tortoise explained that he had been sent as emissary by the gods. The king at once invited him into the palace, and there begged him to explain why his builders had not been able to construct the ramparts to stay.

The golden tortoise answered, "This is a land of rivers and mountains, both inhabited by spirits. It is the spirits of the mountains that are causing your ramparts to collapse. The spirits of the waters remain friendly to you."

With the advice of the golden tortoise, An Duong was then able to triumph over the sorcery of the unfriendly spirits, and he rebuilt his fortifications rapidly. They comprised three enclosures, which extended over a thousand *truong* and twisted about in such a way that they resembled a seashell or conch. So the city was called Co Loa Thanh, the City of the Seashell.

When the city and its fortifications were complete, the golden tortoise took his leave of the king. The latter thanked him profusely for his assistance, led him outside the gates, and said to him, "Thanks to you this city has become powerful. But what will happen when you are gone? Shall I be able to defend it?"

The golden tortoise answered, "Fortune and misfortune depend upon the will of heaven. But if men are deserving, heaven will help them. Since you show such great confidence in me, I can make you a present which will help you. But never forget that it is your own obligation constantly to guard the security of your kingdom."

Whereupon the tortoise broke off one of his own claws and handed it to the king, saying, "Fasten this to your crossbow as a trigger. When you go into combat, you will then be invincible. But remember your own responsibility, and be ever alert!"

Having thus spoken, the golden tortoise turned away toward the river. The king followed him with his eyes until he had entirely disappeared from view beneath the water.

At that time there was reigning in China the powerful

Tan Thuy Hoang, whom the Chinese call Ch'in Shih-huang-ti or First Emperor of the Ch'in Dynasty. He had conquered all his weaker neighbors and had extended his military power as far as the South Seas. Within his own country, this great ruler had achieved unity and over-thrown feudal restraints. In the same year in which he be-gan the construction of the Great Wall, he sent his mighty forces south to attack the kingdom of Au Lac. But, led by their king with his magic crossbow, the warriors of Au Lac were able to hurl back the great Chinese armies even before they approached.

Three years later, this emperor entrusted five hundred thousand men to General Trieu Da, who invaded the lands of Au Lac, where he deployed his troops on the Mountain of the Rusted Axe and his junks on the river.

King An Duong set out from the city at the head of his soldiers to meet the challenge. He lifted his crossbow with its magic claw and hurled three shafts at the invaders. In a trice thirty thousand Chinese bodies were scattered on the ground. The rest of the invaders stampeded in their haste to flee.

Unable to fight against a secret, magic weapon, General Trieu Da decided on a ruse in order to conquer Au Lac. As a first step in his plan, he asked for peace, and sent his own son, Trong Thuy, to the court of the king as pledge of his sincere desire for friendly relations.

The king gave Trieu Da the land situated north of the Bang Giang River. He admitted Trong Thuy to his en-tourage, and finally, captivated by the young man's charm and seeming integrity, gave him the hand of his only daugh-ter, the beautiful Princess My Chau, "Sweetness of the Pearl."

Trong Thuy loved his wife dearly; yet he never forgot the mission with which his father had entrusted him. And Princess My Chau returned his love with all her heart. In response to his pleas, she even showed him, unsuspectingly, the sacred, magic crossbow. Trong Thuy examined the claw with great curiosity and interest. Subsequently he had a duplicate of it made, and he secretly replaced the real claw with the imitation.

Once the magic claw was safe in his possession, Trong Thuy obtained the king's permission to return for a time to his own country. To his wife he explained, "Even the beauty of married love should not cause me to neglect my filial duties toward my parents. It is now a very long time since I have prostrated myself before them." He added that he regretted very much not being able to take her along, but that the road up to the northern lands was long and rough, and that it crossed forests and mountains inhabited by wild beasts. It would not be safe for her to be along.

But, at the moment of parting, he was overcome by a deep emotion when he looked at his lovely wife, who, in her love for him and her trust in him, had unknowingly betrayed her father and her country. On her part, My Chau noted Trong Thuy's great sadness, and she sensed that it was too great for a simple leave-taking. She had a presentiment of misfortune.

She said to him, "The affection of married couples may well be imperishable, but peace between nations is, alas, often ephemeral. It may happen that the North and the South will go to war again. If, one day, I should have to leave this city hurriedly, I shall carry with me the cloak of double-brocaded goose down and feathers which you brought to me from your country. And I shall scatter the feathers along the path by which I flee, to show you the route I have taken."

Trong Thuy hastened to rejoin his father and delivered the miraculous claw to him. General Trieu Da immediately marched once more against King An Duong.

The latter was relaxing over a game of chess when the tidings of a new invasion were brought to him. He received the report with shouts of laughter. And he permitted the enemy to approach, without going out to stop them or taking any measures to defend his capital. Finally a sentry, from the heights of the ramparts, discerned the great mass of the Chinese army darkening the horizon.

The king contented himself with saying, "So, has my bold neighbor forgotten about my crossbow?" And, with that, he went back to his game of chess.

At last, with the enemy at the gates of the city, the king stood up and seized his bow. But when he loosed the first bolt, he realized that he had been betrayed. He had only time to jump on his horse, carrying his daughter behind him, and flee to the south, abandoning his capital and his kingdom.

Entering the defeated city with his father's troops, Trong Thuy searched the palace in vain for his wife. Noticing the trail of feathers which, true to her promise, she had strewn behind her, Trong Thuy threw himself in hot pursuit of the fleeing king and Princess My Chau.

In the meantime the king was crossing plains and jungles like a whirlwind, scaling hills, hurrying down declines, crossing rivers. Each time he stopped he heard the oncoming gallop of his pursuers. And he spurred his horse again, taking up his mad flight in greater haste.

My Chau cowered against her father's back, now encircling with her arms the majestic body that she had not embraced since her early childhood, now freeing herself enough to drop some feathers along the way. Even the wind whipping across her face could not altogether dry her tears. She felt herself a weak, helpless woman, battered by an immense grief.

Finally, the road ended at the edge of the sea. But there was no ship in sight.

"Heaven has abandoned me!" cried the king. "Oh, ambassador of the Limpid Waters, wherever you may be, come quickly to my aid!"

At once the golden tortoise emerged to the top of the sea and cried out in a voice so powerful that Trong Thuy heard it from afar and stopped to listen, "How can you escape an enemy that you carry behind you?"

The king turned around toward his daughter, who could only raise her tear-filled eyes to heaven, without saying anything. Quickly drawing his great sword, shaped like a flame, An Duong cut off his daughter's head. Then he followed the golden tortoise, which opened a path in the waters for him, and disappeared beneath the sea.

When Trong Thuy discovered My Chau's body, he fell from his horse and lifted it in his arms, weeping. And he bore it away for burial in the City of the Seashell.

Then, inconsolable, he wandered all day in the places that had been familiar to his wife. Finally, in a fit of despair, he threw himself into the pool of water where she had loved to bathe in the days of their happiness.

And it is also said that the blood which ran from My Chau's body at the moment of her death stained red the sea at that spot, and that since that time the oysters there have produced precious pearls of a wonderful pink luster. Pearls are also said to assume a marvelous luster when washed in the pool where Trong Thuy drowned himself, where Princess My Chau used to bathe. For does her name not indeed mean Sweetness of the Pearl?

Rajah Soliman's Daughter
Philippines

Rajah Soliman was a renowned warrior—a legend in his lifetime for the bravery with which he defended Manila against the Spaniards in their first attempts to capture the capital city of the Philippines. A great patriot and leader, the Rajah was devoted to his family—especially his only daughter, the charming princess Solimya.

Everyone in Manila had heard of the great beauty of Princess Solimya. In fact, she was the most perfect embodiment of Filipino womanhood, purity and gracefulness. It was but natural that a host of suitors competed with one another for her hand in marriage. Not a few were prepared to pledge their devotion to her for life. The snag was that she did not like any one among them.

As for Rajah Soliman, the princess was the apple of his eye. Loving her with all his life, he lavished every attention on her, all the time ensuring that her every need was provided. In filial devotion, she responded to her father's sentiments, and, as was the custom, obeyed his wishes and commands implicitly.

Princess Solimya went to take her daily bath in the Pasig River. As usual, she was accompanied by her maids. Unknown to her, a young man was fishing nearby, concealed from her view by bushes and trees on the bank of the river. Hearing the sound of the splashes in the water, caused by the princess and the girls, the young man saw them from his hiding place. Noticing the princess, the prettiest and loveliest among the girls, he fell in love with her.

He came again and again to this fishing spot to take a look at the princess. The day came when he could hold himself no more and appeared before her when she had put on her clothes after the bath in the river. In his simple way, he had suffered since he had his first glimpse of her. He told her how he had happened to see her while he was fishing, that he was no Peeping Tom or evil-minded spy but truly and everlastingly in love with her.

Princess Solimya understood him and did not blame him. Their eyes met as she listened to his simple explanation. She, too, fell in love with him and agreed to meet him at this rendezvous. Their love trysts continued, in secret, at the same place.

What the two lovers thought was a closely-guarded secret leaked out. The rumor reached the ears of Rajah Soliman. He could not believe his ears that his dear daughter could have a clandestine love affair behind his back. He found out through his spies who the youth was.

When Rajah Soliman came to know that his daughter's lover was the son of a rival chieftain, his blood boiled for revenge and retribution. He ordered his warriors to capture the young man. Before the lover knew what was happening, he was arrested by the strong men of the Rajah. When he knew who these were, he yielded without resistance. In any case, he was powerless in their hands.

The lover of Princess Solimya knew what to expect from his father's enemy. His only solace was that he would have one last glimpse of the princess in her palace before his death.

The Rajah held a summary trial in his court. He was himself the judge, the final arbiter. As was expected, the sentence was the prisoner's death. It was spelled out as death by drowning before sunrise on the following day. The Rajah further decreed that the prisoner be bound and put in a sack fastened to a rock which would weigh him down when he would be thrown into the Pasig River.

The young man heard the dire verdict and resigned himself to his fate, as he saw Princess Solimya for the last time. Crying and sobbing, she was led away from the courtroom by her maids.

Little did the maids know that the princess was not resigned to her fate. She went on crying until she could not resist the impulse to meet her lover for the last time. She managed to find her way to the cellar where he was kept in the sack. She whispered to her lover, "My dear, I am here to replace you. It is my father who has unjustly ordered your death by drowning. I am the cause of it all. I am the one who should meet that fate."

From inside the sack, her lover, moved by her devotion unto the last, replied, "My dear princess, your grief is painful to me. I cannot, I am sorry, agree to your plan. You know, I cannot live without you."

"No, you have to agree," she protested. The argument went on between the lovers, without any conclusion.

With no agreement in sight, Princess Solimya forced herself into the sack with her lover. She remained there with him, held tight in his embrace.

At the appointed time, well before sunrise, the jailors of Rajah Soliman appeared in the cellar. They carried the sack, tied as it was to the rock, and threw it into the Pasig River. Inside the sack, unknown to the men, were the two lovers, who went down to their doom, without any word or struggle. They sealed the feud of their fathers with their great love and ultimate sacrifice.

It did not take long for the Rajah to discover that his dear daughter had drowned herself with her lover. He was in a panic and ordered his men to recover the sack and save the lovers. But the lovers were already dead when the sack was retrieved.

Rajah Soliman and his family were shocked at the tragedy. Grieving, he addressed the lifeless lovers: "You have proved me wrong. Forgive me. You two were right. I know now that nothing can stand in the way of true love. You will be together evermore."

The Rajah had them accoutred in royal robes and put in a wide coffin side by side. The royal rites of burial were administered to them, as the coffin was lowered in a single grave.

The two lovers lay in eternal rest adjacent to each other. As for their feuding fathers, they were reunited, and jointly fought against their common enemy.

Magic Gifts

In the ordinary world our abilities are finite, our circum-
stances limited, our daily tasks often routine. But the human imagination is not bound by ordinary restraints, and
asks the question, "What if?" What if I did not have to
work so hard to eke out a living? What if I could have anything I wanted just by speaking its name? What if I could
travel anywhere, or become invisible? The human will is
not satisfied with physical limitations and says "I wish!" I
wish I had a magic sword which would kill my enemies, or
a wine jug which would never be empty, or a tree which
would bear coins of gold and silver!

Such wishes come true in popular stories of magic gifts.
The gifts appear in a variety of ways. Sometimes they are
bestowed by a supernatural being or an apparently ordinary being with supernatural powers; sometimes they are
found or stolen; sometimes they are revealed in a dream. In
the first story in this section, the younger brother is not actually given a gift, but takes a magic club left by some gob-

linlike creatures called *tokkaebi*. In the next story, Ma Liang receives a magic brush from an old man with a white beard, while the tavern keeper in "The Dog and the Cat" receives a magic piece of amber from a stranger. Babakud seeks and finds a magic flower after learning of it in a dream; and in other stories people receive aid from birds and insects, and from the Buddhist Goddess of Mercy.

Often a moral element is woven into the story—the gifts come as a reward for hard work, kindness, faithfulness, or other virtues; but people who use the magic gifts for selfish ends are always punished. One can see the results of misuse of magic in "The Tongue-Cut Sparrow," "The Magic Cap," and "The Man in the Moon," while in "Planting Pears" magic is used against a selfish man.

The Tokkaebi's Club
Korea

Long, long ago there were two brothers who lived in a small mountain village. The oldest was wealthy and very selfish and irresponsible while the youngest was poor and very kind and diligent.

Younger Brother took care of his elderly parents because Older Brother refused, even though it was his duty as the oldest son. Every day Younger Brother went into the forest to gather wood to sell in order to buy food for them.

One day he went deeper into the forest than usual. He worked hard most of the morning and afternoon for the ground was covered with fallen branches. He gathered the branches into piles, thinking that he would collect them in the next few days. Finally he sat down to rest with his back against a tree and was soon dozing.

Plop! Something hit the top of his head.

"What was that?" he said, rubbing his head. Then he noticed a hazelnut on the ground beside him. "Oh, this will be a tasty treat for Father," he said, picking it up and putting it into his pocket.

He leaned back against the tree and thought about how happy his father would be to get the tasty nut. Then another nut fell on the ground beside him. "That's good," he told himself, picking it up, "I'll give this one to Mother." A few minutes later, two nuts fell at the same time. "I'll take these to my brother and his wife," he said, picking them up. Another fell and he picked it up, saying, "This one is for me."

He looked up at the top of the tree and saw that the sky was filled with dark clouds. Quickly he gathered up his things and headed down the trail. But he had not gone very far when big rain drops began pelting him. "I'd better take shelter somewhere," he said. "I'll never make it down the mountain in this rain."

After what seemed like hours, he spotted a rundown house a short distance from the path. At the edge of the clearing he called, "Anyone home?" But there was no answer. When he got closer, he realized that it was an abandoned house and very dilapidated. He went inside and lay down on the floor. He fell asleep immediately.

Hours later he was awakened by the sound of loud laughter and talking. "Who could that be?" he asked himself. "Perhaps they're a band of thieves. I must hide!" He looked around the room but could see no hiding place. As the voices came closer, he climbed up into the rafters. He was just positioning himself on a beam when the owners of the voices stomped into the room below.

He peered down carefully. He was so shocked he almost

fell off the beam. There were several horned goblins which he knew at once must be the *tokkaebis* of which he had heard about all his life.

The *tokkaebis* sat and talked for a short time, each relating what kind of tricks he had played on humans that day. Then they began to sing and dance, laughing boisterously all the while. Every now and then they banged their clubs on the floor and chanted, "Thump! Thump! Come out gold! Thump! Thump! Come out silver!" and gold and silver coins poured out of the clubs.

"I'm thirsty," said one of them.

"Then let's have some wine!" shouted the others in unison.

"Thump! Thump! Come out wine! Thump! Thump! Come out wine!" they all chanted and several jugs of wine appeared. They drank the wine and called forth more. Then one of them suggested they have some food. "Thump! Thump! Come out rice! "Thump! Thump! Come out meat!" They banged their clubs over and over until there was an elaborate meal before them.

Younger Brother became very hungry watching the *tokkaebis* eat. Then he remembered the hazelnuts in his pocket. He put one in his mouth and bit down hard. *Cuuraack!*

"What was that?" asked one of the *tokkaebis*.

"The roof is falling!" cried another.

"Let's get out of here!" they all shouted at once and rushed out the door.

Younger Brother was also frightened. He lay where he was until sunup. Then he climbed down from the rafters and looked around inside and outside the house to make sure the *tokkaebis* were gone.

"Am I hungry!" he said, sitting down to the feast the *tokkaebis* left. After eating his fill, he gathered up the gold and silver coins scattered all over the floor and found one of the *tokkaebi*'s clubs standing in a corner of the room. "I wonder," he said, smiling.

Bang! He hit the floor with the club and said, "Thump! Thump! Come out gold!" and gold coins immediately rattled out. "Thump! Thump! Come out clothes!" he said, and a set of clothes appeared. "Thump! Thump! Come out rice!" he said, and rice appeared.

Younger Brother hurried home to his worried parents. They rejoiced at their good fortune. He bought some land with the gold and silver coins and built a fine house. He used the club to provide whatever food, clothes, and other necessities he and his parents needed.

It wasn't long before Older Brother heard that his brother had become wealthy overnight and decided he should go see for himself. When he heard about the *tokkaebi*'s club, he decided that he had to have one, too. So the next day he set out for the shack in the forest. He stopped to rest under the hazelnut tree and daydreamed about how rich he was going to be when he got a *tokkaebi*'s club.

He collected some nuts for his parents and his wife and children but then ate them himself. When the sun started getting low, he put a few nuts in his pocket and headed for the shack. He found it with no problem and went inside and climbed up into the rafters to wait for the *tokkaebis* to come. Just when he decided they were not coming, he heard loud laughter.

They came noisily into the house and sat down. They talked about their day's activities and then began playing games with their clubs. Older Brother became so excited at seeing gold and silver coins pour out of the clubs that he took out a hazelnut and crunched down on it with his teeth.

The *tokkaebis* stopped dancing.

"Did you hear that?" asked one.

"Yes," said the others.

"It must be that guy who tricked us last time and made off with my club," said another with a scowl on his face.

"Let's get him!" shouted the others.

The *tokkaebis* began searching the place. Older Brother was so scared his teeth began to chatter.

"There he is," one of them shouted, pointing to the ceiling. "Get him!"

In the blink of an eye, Older Brother found himself on the floor. "No, no. Don't hurt me. Please let me go. Please," he cried, rubbing his hands together.

But the *tokkaebis* just laughed. "Thump! Thump! Beat him up! Beat the thief who stole our club!" they chanted and banged their clubs on the floor. All night they toyed with Older Brother, over and over tickling him, beating him and stretching and shrinking his ears, arms, legs, neck, and nose. At the crack of dawn, they disappeared into the forest.

Older Brother finally managed to stand up but he fell over immediately because his nose was so long he could not balance. After several attempts, he succeeded in balancing himself by supporting his nose with his hands. He tried to sneak home but many a villager saw him.

When word of what happened to his brother reached Younger Brother, he took his club and went to his brother's house. "Thump! Thump! Go back in! Make his nose short again!" he said, banging the club on the floor, and Older Brother's nose was the size it had been.

"Thank you, thank you," cried Older Brother. "Please forgive me for all the bad things I have done. I want to be good and kind like you. I want to be a good brother and a good son." And from then on, he was.

Ma Liang and His Magic Brush
China

Once upon a time there was a boy named Ma Liang, whose father and mother had died when he was a child, so that he had to earn his living by gathering firewood and cutting weeds. Ma Liang was a very clever boy and longed to learn to paint, but he could not afford to buy even one brush.

One day Ma Liang passed a private school while the schoolmaster was painting, and was fascinated to watch the strokes made by his brush. Before he knew it he had slipped into the school.

"I want so much to learn to paint," he said. "Please, will you lend me a brush?"

"What!" The master glared at him. "A little beggar wants to paint? You must be dreaming!" He drove the lad away.

But Ma Liang had a will of his own.

"Why shouldn't I learn to paint even if I am poor?" he said to himself.

He made up his mind to learn, and practiced hard every day. When he went up the mountain to gather firewood, he would use a twig to draw birds on the sand; when he went to the river to cut reeds, he would dip his finger into the water and trace fish on the rock; when he got home, he would sketch his few sticks of furniture on the walls of his cave, until soon the four walls were covered with his drawings.

Time passed quickly, and since Ma Liang did not let a single day go by without practicing drawing, naturally he made rapid progress. People who saw his pictures almost expected the birds to warble and the fish to swim, they were so true to life. But still Ma Liang had no brush! He often thought how happy he would be if he could have one.

One night, tired out after working and drawing all day, Ma Liang fell fast asleep as soon as he lay down on his pallet. Then an old man with a long white beard appeared to him and gave him a brush.

"This is a magic brush," said the old man. "Use it carefully!"

Ma Liang took the brush in his hand. It was of glittering gold and rather heavy.

"What a beautiful brush!" He jumped for joy. "Thank you ever so much . . ."

Before Ma Liang could finish thanking him, the old man with the white beard vanished. The lad woke with a start. So it was a dream! But how could it be a dream when the magic brush was there in his hand? He was lost in wonder.

He painted a bird with this magic brush, and the bird flapped its wings, then soared up into the sky where it began to sing merrily for him to hear. He painted a fish with his magic brush, and the fish frisked its tail, then plunged into the river and sported in the water for him to see. He was in rapture.

With this magic brush, Ma Liang painted every day for the poor folk in his village: a plough, a hoe, an oil lamp, or a bucket, for whichever family had none. But no secret can be kept forever. The news of Ma Liang's magic brush soon reached the ears of a rich landlord in that village, and the landlord sent two of his men to seize Ma Liang and force the boy to paint for him.

Though Ma Liang was only a lad, he had plenty of courage. He had seen through those rich people, and no matter how the landlord threatened or flattered him, he refused to paint a single picture. So the landlord shut him up in a stable and began to starve him.

Three days later it began to snow heavily, and by the evening snow lay thick on the ground. Thinking that Ma Liang must have died of cold if not of hunger by now, the landlord went to the stable to look. As he approached the door he saw red firelight shining through its chinks and sniffed a delicious smell of food. And peeping through a crack in the door, what should he see but Ma Liang toasting himself by a big stove and eating hot cakes! The landlord could hardly believe his eyes. Where had the stove and cakes come from? Then he realized that Ma Liang must have painted them. Trembling with rage, he summoned his men to kill Ma Liang and seize the magic brush.

But by the time a dozen of his fiercest men rushed into the stable, Ma Liang was nowhere to be seen—all they found was a ladder leaning against the wall by which Ma Liang had made his escape. The landlord lost no time in mounting the ladder in pursuit, but he tumbled and fell before he reached the third rung. And when he got to his feet again, the ladder had vanished.

After escaping from the landlord's house Ma Liang knew he could not hide in the village, for that would only get the friends who sheltered him into trouble. He must go far away. He waved farewell to the familiar cottages, murmuring, "Good-bye, dear friends!"

Then he painted a fine horse, mounted it and galloped down the highway.

He had not gone far when he heard a hubbub behind him, and turning his head saw the landlord and nearly a score of his lackeys pursuing him on horseback. They carried bright torches, and a sword flashed in the landlord's hand.

Soon they were quite near. Calmly, Ma Liang drew a bow and an arrow with his magic brush, and fitted the arrow to the bow. "Whiz!" The arrow pierced the landlord's throat and he fell headlong from his horse. Then Ma Liang lashed his own steed so that it flew forward as if on wings.

Ma Liang galloped down the highway for several days and nights without stopping, till he came to a town and decided to stay there, for he was now far, far away from his native village. Since he could find no work in that town, he had to paint pictures and sell them in the market. But in order that he might not be discovered, he took care not to let his pictures come to life by drawing birds without a beak or animals with one leg missing.

One day, after painting a crane with no eyes, he was careless enough to splash ink on the bird's head where the eyes should have been, whereupon the crane opened its eyes, flapped it wings and flew off. At once the whole town was agog with excitement. And some busybody reported it to the emperor, who sent officers to summon Ma Liang to court. Ma Liang had no wish to go, but with promises and veiled threats they carried him off.

Ma Liang had heard many stories about the emperor's cruelty to the poor, and hated him from the bottom of his heart. He was certainly not going to serve such a man. So when the emperor ordered him to paint a dragon, he painted a toad instead; when the emperor ordered him to paint a phoenix, he painted a cock instead. This ugly toad and filthy cock leaped and flapped around the emperor, leaving dirt and droppings everywhere, till the whole palace stank. Then the emperor, in a towering rage, ordered his guards to seize the magic brush from Ma Liang and throw him into prison.

Now that the emperor had this magic brush, he tried painting with it himself. First he painted a gold mountain. Then, thinking one gold mountain was not enough, he added another and yet another, until his picture was a mass of mountains. But when the painting was finished, what do you think happened to those gold mountains? They turned into a pile of rocks. And because they were top-heavy, they toppled down, nearly crushing the emperor's feet in their fall.

Still the emperor was not cured of his greed. Having

failed to paint gold mountains, he decided to paint gold bricks. He painted a brick, but it seemed too small. He painted a bigger one, but still it seemed too small. Finally he painted a long, long golden bar. But when the picture was finished, what do you think happened? The golden bar turned into an enormous python, which rushed at him with its huge, crimson mouth wide open, and the emperor fainted from fear. Luckily, his officers were quick in coming to the rescue, otherwise he would have been swallowed by the terrible monster.

Finding he could make no use of the magic brush himself, the emperor released Ma Liang and spoke to him amicably, presenting him with gold and silver and promising to give him a princess in marriage. Ma Liang, who had already formed a plan, pretended to agree to all these proposals. Then the emperor was very pleased and returned the magic brush to him.

"If he paints a mountain," thought the emperor, "wild beasts may come out of it. Better paint the sea!"

So he ordered Ma Liang to paint the sea first.

Ma Liang took up his magic brush, and sure enough, a clear, boundless sea appeared before the emperor. Its blue surface was unruffled and it shone like an immense jade mirror.

"Why are there no fish in this sea?" asked the emperor, looking at it.

Ma Liang made a few dots with his magic brush, whereupon fish of all the colors of the rainbow appeared. Frisking their tails, they sported merrily for a while, then swam slowly far out to sea.

The emperor had been watching them with the greatest pleasure, so as they swam farther and farther away he urged Ma Liang, "Hurry up and paint a boat! I want to sail out to sea to watch those fish."

Ma Liang painted a huge sailing boat, upon which the

121

emperor and empress, princes, princesses and many ministers embarked. Then, with a few strokes, he drew wind.
Fine ripples appeared on the sea and the boat moved off.

But the emperor found the pace too slow. Standing at the
bow, he shouted, "Let the wind blow harder! Harder!"

A few powerful strokes from Ma Liang's magic brush
brought a strong wind. The sea grew rough, and the white
sails billowed out as the boat scudded toward mid-ocean.

Ma Liang drew a few more strokes. Then the sea roared,
big waves rolled, and the vessel began to keel over.

"That's enough wind!" shouted the emperor at the top of
his voice. "Enough, I say!"

But Ma Liang paid no attention. He continued to wield
his magic brush. The sea was lashed into fury and billows
broke over the deck.

The emperor, drenched through, clung to the mast,
shaking his fist at Ma Liang and shouting.

Ma Liang, however, pretended to hear nothing, and
went on drawing wind. A hurricane blew black clouds before it to darken the sky, and angry billows reared themselves higher and higher to crash down one after the other
on the boat. At last the vessel keeled over, capsized and
broke up. The emperor and his ministers sank to the bottom of the sea.

After the emperor's death, the story of Ma Liang and his
magic brush spread far and wide. But what became of Ma
Liang? Nobody knows for certain.

Some say that he went back to his native village and rejoined his peasant companions.

Others say that he roamed the earth, painting for the
poor wherever he went.

The Tongue-cut Sparrow
Japan

Well, this was long ago. There were an old man and his wife. One day the old man went to the mountains to cut firewood. When he got there he hung his lunch on the branch of a tree, and a sparrow came along and ate it up. When the old man got ready to eat his lunch, he unwrapped it and found the sparrow in it, asleep. He took the sparrow and cared for it. He named it Ochon.

One day the old man left the sparrow with the old woman and went to the mountains to cut firewood. Since it was a nice day, the old woman decided to do her washing, and so she made some starch. She said to the sparrow, "I am going to the river to do the washing; you watch the starch so that the neighbor's cat doesn't get into it," and she went off to the river.

The sparrow became very hungry, so it ate up all the starch. When the old woman returned from the river, she asked, "Ochon, Ochon, what happened to the starch?"

"The neighbor's cat ate it," replied the sparrow.

The old woman looked in the neighbor's cat's mouth, but there was no trace of starch there. Then she looked in the sparrow's mouth, and saw some starch stuck there. She cut out the sparrow's tongue and drove the poor sparrow out of the house.

Soon the old man returned from the mountains and asked "Where is Ochon?"

"I made some starch," said the old woman, "but while I was at the river, the sparrow ate it up. I got angry and cut out its tongue and drove it away."

The old man felt sorry for the sparrow and went off to hunt for it, calling out,

123

Where has Ochon the sparrow gone?
Where has the tongue-cut sparrow gone?
The poor little thing, where has he gone?

He went for some distance and came to a man who was washing cows. "Cow-washer-sama, cow-washer-sama, a tongue-cut sparrow didn't come by here, did he?"

"He came by, he came by. If you'll drink the cow's wash water, out of father's bowl filled thirteen times and out of mother's bowl filled thirteen times, I'll tell you where he went."

The old man drank the cow's wash water and was told, "Go on down the road and you will come to a horse-washer."

Where has the tongue-cut sparrow gone?
Where has Ochon the sparrow gone?
The poor little thing, the poor little thing!

Singing this song, the old man went along for some way and came to a horse-washer. "Horse-washer-sama, horse-washer-sama, a tongue-cut sparrow didn't come by here, did he?"

"He came by, he came by. If you'll drink the horse's wash water, out of father's bowl filled thirteen times and out of mother's bowl filled thirteen times, I'll tell you where he went."

The old man drank the horse's wash water and was told, "Go on down the road and you will come to a greens-washer."

Where has Ochon the sparrow gone?
Where has the tongue-cut sparrow gone?
The poor little thing, the poor little thing!

The old man went for some way and came to a greens-washer. "Greens-washer-sama, greens-washer-sama, a tongue-cut sparrow didn't come by here, did he?"

"He came by, he came by. If you'll drink the water I washed greens in, out of mother's bowl filled thirteen times and out of father's bowl filled thirteen times, I'll tell you where he went."

The old man drank the water the greens had been washed in and was told, "Go on down this road and you will come to a large bamboo grove. Go into the grove, and there the sparrow will be. He will have on a red apron and a red sleeve binder and will be cutting rice."

Where has the tongue-cut sparrow gone?
Where has Ochon the sparrow gone?
The poor little thing, the poor little thing!

The old man sang this song as he went along. He went for quite some way and finally came to a large bamboo grove. He went into the grove and soon came to the sparrow's house. He knocked at the door, and a voice called, "Is it grandfather or grandmother?"

"It's grandfather, it's grandfather."

"Then if it's grandfather, come right on in."

When the old man went in, he was given a feast and was well entertained. Then the sparrow asked, "Would you like to have a heavy trunk or a light one?"

"I am getting old; I would rather have the light one," he said, and so the light trunk was put on the old man's shoulders. "You must not open this until you get home. Then you may open it," he was told.

When the old man got home, he opened the trunk and found to his and the old woman's joy that it was full of *oban* and *koban* coins.

The old woman was very greedy and said, "I shall go and

get some too." She set off, and when she got to the sparrow's place, she knocked on the door. A voice came, "Is it grandfather or grandmother?"

"It's grandmother, it's grandmother."

"Then if it's grandmother, come right on in."

The old woman went in and instead of a tray, she was served on a board from the toilet. Sticks were broken off the fence for her to use as chopsticks, and she was given sand instead of rice.

When the old woman was ready to leave, she was asked, "Grandmother, would you rather have a heavy basket or a light one?" Since she was very greedy, she replied that she would take the heavy one. "Then take it on your shoulders and do not look inside until you get home," the sparrow said.

The old woman wanted to peek in the basket, so she went behind the fence and opened it up. When she did that, snakes and vipers and scorpions came out and stung the old woman to death.

We should not be greedy.

Little One Inch
Japan

Once long ago, in a certain place there lived a man and his wife who loved one another very much. They had no children, but they wanted one so badly they said that even a child as small as the end of a finger would be all right. One day they went to the shrine of Sumiyoshi-sama and prayed with all their might, "Sumiyoshi-sama, please give us a child, even if it is only as big as the end of a finger."

Now it happened that ten months after this, a charming little baby boy was born. The baby, however, was so tiny that it was only as large as the end of a finger, so they named him Issun Boshi, "Little One Inch." They raised him with loving care, but no matter how much time passed, he never grew any bigger at all. One day they decided to give him a sewing needle as a sword and send him away from home.

There was nothing else Little One Inch could do, so he took the rice bowl and chopsticks his mother gave him and set off. He used the rice bowl as a boat and the chopsticks as oars and started off for the capital city. After many, many days he finally arrived at the emperor's capital. He walked about here and there, and after a while he stopped in front of a splendid big house. He went into the entrance hall of the house and called as loud as he could, "I beg indulgence, I beg indulgence!"

The people of the house thought it a strange-sounding voice and, wondering who it was, went to the entrance hall to see. There they saw the tiny little boy standing under the wooden clogs. "Little boy, was it you who called just now?" they asked.

"Yes, it was; I am called Little One Inch. I have been sent away from home by my parents. Would you please take me into your house?" They thought him interesting, so they decided to take care of him. Little One Inch was small, but he was very clever. Whatever they asked him, he knew much more, and soon everyone was calling, "Little One Inch, Little One Inch," because they loved him so much. The daughter of the house, especially, came to be very fond of him.

One day she took Little One Inch with her and went to pray to the goddess Kannon. On the way back, two *oni* met them. They were just about to seize the girl when Little One Inch drew the needle from its scabbard at his waist and brandishing it about, cried as loud as he could, "I don't know who you think I am. Well, I am Little One Inch who has accompanied the master's daughter on a pilgrimage to Kannon-sama!" In spite of this, one of the *oni* took Little One Inch and swallowed him whole. Since Little One Inch was so small, he could move about easily in the *oni*'s stomach. Waving his sword about, he danced around puncturing the *oni*'s stomach. The *oni* was so surprised that he coughed Little One Inch up and spit him out. Then the other *oni* grabbed him and was going to crush him, but Little One Inch saw his chance and jumped into the *oni*'s eye. The *oni*'s eye hurt so that both the *oni* ran away.

Little One Inch started home with the girl, who all this time had been standing to one side shaking with fright. Just as they set off, they saw a little hammer that had been dropped along the way. The girl picked it up, and Little One Inch asked what it was. The girl said, "This is a magic striking hammer. No matter what you want, you can strike with the hammer and you will get it."

"Then please strike me with it and see if you can make me grow taller, will you," asked Little One Inch. The girl waved the hammer and cried, "Grow taller, grow taller," and to their surprise Little One Inch's body began to grow and grow until soon he became a splendid young samurai.

Umpong-Umpong and Babakud
Malaysia

Once upon a time, there was a cave in the middle of a deep forest near Mount Tadusmadi, where an old woman lived quite alone, for she was an enchantress. During the day she changed herself into a wild cat or an owl, but in the evening she became an ordinary woman again. She was able to entice birds and animals to come to her cave, and she would kill and cook them.

If any youth found himself within a hundred yards of the cave, he became rooted to the spot and could not stir until the woman set him free. If a pretty girl came inside that magic circle, the old enchantress changed her into a bird and locked her up in a strong bamboo cage. She had ten thousand such cages in the cave, each containing a rare bird that had once been a happy, carefree young village girl.

Now there was once a maiden called Umpong-Umpong, who was very beautiful. She was betrothed to a youth named Babakud, and their greatest delight was to be together. One summer evening the two went for a walk in the forest. It was calm and peaceful under the trees, and the fading sunlight glinted on the dark green leaves. "How beautiful this place is!" sighed Babakud. "But we must be careful not to come too close to the witch's cave."

They wandered on, hand in hand, and without knowing why, they began to feel sad and forlorn. In a nearby tree a hornbill sang its plaintive lament. They looked around, quite confused, for they did not remember their way home. Umpong-Umpong began to weep and sob, overcome by a strange fear. Babakud tried to comfort her, but he, too, felt something ominous in the atmosphere around them.

Half the sun was still above the mountain and half had dropped behind it when Babakud looked through the trees and saw the huge entrance to the witch's cave near them. He was terrified. In the last rays of the setting sun, Umpong-Umpong sank to the ground and began to sing:

Tombolog Tokoroh Ku Aragang Kopizoh Oh Liaw Limbai . . .

> Tosusah, Tosusah, Tosusah; Lumimbai ehzaw di
> Kukuruk
> Todoroh Napatai, Limbai Tosusah . . . Ohwow,
> Ohwow, Ohwow!

Babakud looked at Umpong-Umpong. Right before his eyes she was changing into a peacock, and was singing, "Ohwow, Ohwow, Ohwow." An owl with glowing eyes flew three times around her and screeched thrice, "Whook, Whook, Whook!" Babakud could not stir. He stood still like a stone. He could not weep or speak, or move his hand or foot.

Now the sun had disappeared. The owl flew into a bush, and immediately an old bent woman came out of it. She was red-skinned and thin and had large red glowing eyes and a hooked nose which met her chin. She muttered to herself, caught the peacock that had once been Umpong-Umpong, and carried it away in her hand. Babakud stood speechless and motionless until at last the woman returned and said in a gruff voice, "Greetings, young man. When the moon shines on the pot outside my cave you will be freed." And suddenly the moon broke through a cloud and Babakud was free. He fell on his knees before the old woman and begged her to give him back his Umpong-Umpong. She said he would never see Umpong-Umpong again, and then she went away. He called after her; he wept, but it was all in vain. "What is to become of me?" he cried.

After a while he found a way out of the forest and came to a strange village. There he took employment as a keeper of buffaloes and stayed on looking after buffaloes for a long time. He often went back to the cave but never came too close. Then one night he dreamt that he found a blood-red flower, in the center of which was a beautiful pearl. He plucked it and took it with him to the witch's cave. Everything he touched with the flower was freed from the enchantment and thus he rescued his lovely Umpong-Umpong.

When Babakud awoke he set out to find such a flower. He roamed through woods and valleys and crossed steep mountains in his search. For nine days he did not give up hope, and on the tenth, early in the morning, he found it. In the center of this flower was a large dewdrop, as big as the most lovely and expensive pearl. He traveled day and night with the flower until he arrived at the cave. This time, when he came within a hundred yards, he was still able to move, and he continued on till he reached the entrance. Delighted at his success, he touched the great gate with the flower, and it sprang open. He entered, passed through the main opening and then stopped to listen for the singing of the birds.

At last Babakud heard their melodious chirping and followed the sounds until he found himself in the middle of the Great Cave. And there was the enchantress, and with her were thousands of birds in their strong bamboo cages.

When she saw Babakud she flew into a rage and breathed out a poison and blew at him, but she could not move a step towards him. He took no notice of her and looked at the thousands of cages filled with different kinds of birds. How was Babakud to find Umpong-Umpong among them? While he was considering, he saw the ugly old witch pick up a cage and steal towards the door. Babakud sprang after her and touched her and the cage with his flower, making her powerless to work enchantments ever again. Then a peacock stepped out of the bamboo cage, and became Umpong-Umpong, more beautiful than before.

Then Babakud walked all over the cave, touching each cage with his magic flower. One by one the birds were released and turned back into lovely maidens. When they were all freed, Babakud went home with Umpong-Umpong, and they lived a long and happy life.

Planting Pears
China

*Once there was a villager who peddled pears in the market-*place. His pears were fragrant and sweet, and he asked a high price for them. A Daoist priest wearing a tattered head-band and ragged robes was begging in front of the villager's cart, and though the pedlar asked him to leave he would not go away. The pedlar then grew angry and began to swear at him, but the Daoist priest said, "You have several hundred pears on your cart, and I am only asking for one. This would be no great loss to you, so why does it make you so angry?" The bystanders all urged the pedlar to give him one of the less perfect pears, but he adamantly refused. Then a local official, annoyed at the commotion, took out a few coins, bought a pear, and gave it to the priest.

The priest bowed in thanks and said to the crowd, "We men of the cloth do not understand stinginess. Now I have some nice pears here, and I invite you all to share them with me." Someone said, "Since you had some pears, why didn't you eat one of your own?" The priest replied, "I need the seeds from this one to grow them."

Then he ate the pear, keeping one seed in his hand. Untying a pick from his shoulder, he dug a hole several inches deep in the ground, put the seed into the hole, and covered it up with dirt. He asked if someone in the crowd would get him a little hot water to water it with, and when a helpful bystander did fetch some water from a nearby shop, he proceeded to water the seed.

While ten thousand eyes were watching, a sprout began to emerge, growing larger and larger, until it was a fully formed tree. Leaves appeared on its branches, then flowers; then fruit large and fragrant hung heavily all over the tree.

The Daoist priest began to pick the pears and distribute them to the bystanders, and in a moment they had all been given away. Then he took his pick and began to hack at the tree until he had chopped through the trunk. He shouldered the tree, leaves and all, and strolled out of the market.

From the very beginning the villager who peddled pears had joined the crowd, and he had become so absorbed in watching the priest that he forgot about his own business. After the priest had left the marketplace, he turned back to his own cart and discovered that all his pears were missing. Only then did he realize that the pears the priest had given away were his own pears. When he looked more carefully at his cart, he saw that one of the handles had been newly chopped off. In a fiery rage he ran after the priest, and when he turned the corner he found the handle cast away at the foot of a wall, and realized that it was the trunk of the tree the priest had chopped down. The Daoist priest was nowhere to be seen, and the people in the marketplace found the whole incident to be quite entertaining.

The Magic Cap
Korea

The goblins of Korea used to wear magic caps, called Horang Gamte, which had the power of rendering them invisible.

Now once there lived a man who was most diligent in his worship of his ancestors. He was always holding services to their memory, with lavish offerings of delicious food and drink. One day, when he had held such a service, a group of goblins came to his house, and ate up all the good things set

133

out on the altars. And on every following occasion they did the same. Of course they were invisible, for they wore their magic caps, and so the offerings just disappeared. The man was very gratified at first to see his offerings eaten, for it seemed to prove that his ancestors relished them. So he spent more and more money to provide even more lavish feasts until he was almost ruined.

At last his wife complained of his extravagance. "There must be something wrong," she said. "The spirits of our ancestors would never eat so much as to leave us almost ruined. There must be thieves coming in and stealing them while we are occupied with the ceremonial and bowing before the altar. In future I think we ought to keep a careful watch."

So one night the husband hid behind a screen by the altar. He held a stout cudgel in his hand. In the middle of the night he heard the sound of whispering and of food being eaten. He peeped over the screen and saw the food steadily disappearing from the dishes. Yet he could see no one by the table. So all of a sudden he rushed out brandishing his cudgel and rushed round the altar and into all the corners of the room. Alarmed by his violent onslaught the goblins ran away, but the man touched one of them with his cudgel and knocked his cap off. When the goblins had gone the man saw a red cap lying on the floor, the likes of which he had never seen before. He picked it up curiously and put it on, and then began to shout "Thief! Thief!"

His wife heard his shouts and came into the hall. But she could not see her husband, though she could hear him beside her gasping breathlessly, "The thief got away, but he left a very strange cap behind. See?" His wife just stood there bewildered and said, "But where are you, my dear? I can't see you." Her husband took her by the hand and said, "I'm here. What's the matter?" She felt him take hold of her, and tried to grasp him. She chanced to knock off the cap which he had put on his head. No sooner had it fallen to the floor than she saw him standing beside her.

She picked up the cap and said, "Is this the cap you mean? It must have made you invisible. So that's how the thief got in unnoticed. Let me try it." She put it on her head and immediately vanished. "This must be *Horang Gamte,* the magic cap. I'm sure of it!" she exclaimed. "The thief was no man, but a goblin."

Having made this remarkable find they determined that they would turn it to their profit. From that day on they went from house to house in the village, stealing all that they could lay their hands on. Many complaints were made to the authorities, but though a strict watch was kept not a single clue could be found, so stealthily were the thefts committed.

They continued their activities for more than a year, and became very rich. But one day the husband went to a jeweler's shop. It was not open yet, so he waited by the door. In a little while the jeweler came along and opened the door and the thief slipped in behind him. The jeweler took his money from the safe and began to count it. While he was counting it he was amazed to see the coins disappearing one by one. He searched the whole shop, on the floor, and in every corner, but could find no trace of them. Then he looked up, and saw a piece of thread moving slowly in the air. He grabbed it with his fingers, something dropped on the floor, and there beside him he saw a man. The magic cap was beginning to wear out, and a thread had come loose from one of the seams.

The jeweler seized him with both hands, but when he returned all the money he had stolen and offered him the magic cap he let him go. Then the jeweler neglected his business and began himself to use the magic cap as the other had done. One day in the harvest time he went to a rich farmer's house, wearing the magic cap on his head.

The yard was full of laborers threshing rice with flails. As he passed through the yard to the house one of the flails knocked the cap off his head, and it fell in tatters to the ground. So he was discovered, and immediately arrested.

He was brought to trial, and the husband and wife as well. They were all condemned to imprisonment, and shortly afterwards died in prison.

The Wonder-Tree
Indonesia

Once there were three orphan sisters, the two eldest of whom one day found in a harvested field a bird called Kekeko, and bringing it home, they put it in a cage. A few days later they heard the bird call, "Set me in a basket, and I will lay." Though at first they paid no attention, they finally did as it demanded, since it frequently repeated the request; and lo! The next morning the basket was full of cooked rice and fish, steaming hot. This continued daily, and thus the children obtained their food; but as there was always too much in the basket, and it could not be kept, after a while they asked the bird to give them uncooked rice instead. This it did, and before long so great a store of rice was thus accumulated that all who came to the house were amazed at the wealth of provisions which the three poor orphans had.

One day their uncle, who had heard of the great amount of rice possessed by the children, came to visit them. When he asked how they secured their supply, they said, "We have a bird, Kekeko, which we caught, and it gives us all the rice." The jealous uncle asked them to lend him the bird, and they agreed to do so, but first they whispered to it not to give their uncle any rice, or at best a poor grade. This order the bird carried out; but when the uncle saw that the bird failed to give him any rice, in his anger he killed and ate it.

After a time the two oldest orphans, his nieces, came to him to get their bird back, but the uncle said, "He does not exist any longer, for I ate him up." On hearing this, the orphans were sad and rolled on the ground in grief, because they thought that they had lost forever Kekeko, the bird which had helped them. However, they gathered up the bones of the bird and buried them near their house; and lo! From them a wonderful tree soon grew, whose leaves were of silken stuffs, whose blossoms were earrings, and whose fruits produced a pleasing sound. Thus the children were again helped by Kekeko, even after its death.

Serungal
Malaysia

Serungal was an ugly man, but he wished very much to marry a rajah's daughter. On his way to the village of the rajah he saw some men killing an ant, but when he remonstrated with them, they ran away and left the insect, which crawled off in safety. A little farther on Serungal heard some people shouting and found that they were trying to kill a firefly, whose life he saved in the same manner as he had that of the ant; and before he reached the rajah's gate he also rescued a squirrel.

Having arrived before the rajah, Serungal made known to him that he had come to ask for the hand of one of his daughters; but since the rajah did not want him for a son-in-law, he said to him, "If you can pick up the rice which is in this basket, after it has been scattered over the plain, you may have my daughter."

Serungal thought that he could not succeed in this impossible task, for the rajah allowed him only a short time to complete it; but nevertheless he determined to try, only to find that achievement was hopeless. He began to weep, but soon an ant came to him, and learning the reason of his lamentation, said, "Well, stop crying, and I will help you, for you helped me when men wished to kill me." Then the ant called his companions, who quickly sought and gathered the grains of rice, so that the basket soon was full once more.

When Serungal carried the receptacle to the rajah and announced that he had accomplished the task, the latter said, "Well, you may have my daughter, but first you must climb my betel-nut tree and pluck all the nuts." Now this tree was so tall that its top was lost in the clouds, and Serungal, after several vain attempts, sat at the foot of the tree, weeping. To him then came the squirrel whom he had befriended, and in gratitude for the aid which Serungal had given him it climbed the tree for him and brought down all the nuts.

The rajah had one more task, however, for Serungal to accomplish, telling him that he might have his youngest daughter if he could pick her out from among her six other sisters when all were shut up in a perfectly dark room. Serungal again was in despair when the firefly came to him and said, "I will search for you and I will settle on the nose of the seventh daughter, so wherever you see a light, that will be the place where the rajah's youngest daughter is."

So Serungal went into the darkened room, and seeing the

firefly, carried away the woman on whom it had settled. The rajah admitted Serungal's success and thus was obliged to recognize him as his son-in-law.

The Dog and the Cat
Korea

In a small riverside village there lived an old tavern keeper named Ku. He lived alone except for a dog and a cat which never left his side. The dog guarded the door and the cat kept the storeroom free of rats.

Ku was always kind and honest. He was also very poor because, unlike most tavern owners, he was very quiet and did not encourage his customers to drink until they became drunk. He sold only one kind of wine, but it was very good. People would come from the far end of the village to drink it and travelers often asked for a jug to take with them.

But there was something strange about Ku's wine. No matter how much he sold, he never seemed to run out. This was a source of curiosity for Ku's neighbors for they never saw any wine delivered to the tavern and they knew that Ku did not make any. They could not imagine where he obtained his wine. It was a secret that Ku shared only with his dog and cat.

Ku had not always been a tavern keeper. Many years before he had been a ferryman, ferrying people back and forth across the broad river which flowed beside his tavern.

One cold, rainy night, when he had just returned home from making his last run across the river, a stranger knocked at his door. "Please, sir, could you spare a bowl of wine to help take the chill out of these old bones of mine," he asked humbly.

"Come in," said Ku. "My wine jug is almost empty. But you're welcome to drink what's in it." He emptied the contents of his jug into a bowl for the stranger. But the stranger poured a little of it into the jug and then drank thirstily.

"You have been most kind," said the stranger as he got to his feet. "I want you to have this as a token of my appreciation," he said, handing Ku a piece of amber. "Keep it in your wine jug and it will never be dry."

Ku turned the amber over and over in his hands for a while and then, with a laugh, dropped it into his wine jug, thinking he would have to fill it the next day. He ate a few pieces of dried fish and eyed the jug thirstily. "There must be a sip at least," Ku told himself picking up the jug. What a shock! The jug was full.

He poured a bowl and took a small sip. It was the sweetest, richest wine he had ever tasted. He drank a bowl and poured another. But the level of the wine in the jug remained the same.

Ku laughed heartily. "What a wonderful thing! The guy must have been a god! With this I can open a tavern! There will be no more ferrying back and forth across that damn river in all kinds of weather for this old man! I'll open a tavern! That's what I'll do! I will! I will!"

And that's exactly what Ku did and how he came to have an endless supply of wine.

But then one day something terrible happened. Ku picked up his jug to serve a traveler. It was empty. He shook it and shook it but there was not a sound. He was dumbfounded. The traveler left scratching his head as Ku wailed over and over, "It can't be! It can't be! I must have poured it out! I must have poured it into someone's wine bowl or jug! Woe is me! What shall I do?"

The dog and cat shared Ku's sadness. They sniffed all

around the shop to try to find the amber.

"I'm sure I could find it if I could only pick up the scent," the cat told the dog.

"Let's look for it," said the dog. "Let's go through every house in the neighborhood. We must find it. He is so sad and unhappy," he said, looking at Ku.

So they began their search, determined to find the amber for their master. It was difficult and dangerous and took many days but they prowled through every house and shop in the village. They vowed to search the houses on the other side of the river when they could cross. Thus, when the river froze, they crept back and forth. All winter, they crept across to prowl the houses and shops.

At last one day when the river was beginning to thaw, the cat caught the scent of the amber and located it in a document box atop a chest-on-chest. But they didn't know what to do. If the cat pushed the box off the chest, someone would hear them. Moreover, the box was too big for the dog to carry in his mouth.

"Let's ask the rats to help us," suggested the dog. "They can gnaw a hole in the box and get the amber out for us."

"Do you really expect them to help us?" laughed the cat.

"I know it sounds farfetched. But we could promise not to bother them for ten years," said the dog.

"I guess it wouldn't hurt to ask them," said the cat reluctantly. "After all, it seems we have no other choice."

Surprisingly, the rats consented, but then they welcomed the chance to live without having to be afraid of dogs and cats. It took them several days to gnaw a hole large enough for a small rat to go inside the box and carry the amber out in its teeth.

The dog and cat thanked the rats over and over and then headed for the river. They took turns carrying the amber in their mouths.

"Oh no!" cried the cat when they got to the river's edge.

"The ice has melted! How can we get across? You know I can't swim."

"Yes, I know. That's a problem," said the dog. "I know," he said after a while, "I'll carry you on my back and you'll carry the amber in your mouth."

"All right. Let's go," said the cat, and it took the amber in its mouth and climbed onto the dog's back.

The dog walked into the water and began swimming. Presently he said, "Are you holding the amber tightly?"

Of course, with the amber in its mouth, the cat couldn't answer.

A little bit later, the dog again asked, "Do you still have the amber?"

The cat wanted to tell the dog not to worry, but with the amber in its mouth it couldn't.

"Are you holding the amber tightly?" "Have you dropped it?" "Do you have it in your mouth?" The dog asked over and over, and, of course, the cat did not respond. As they came near the riverbank the dog shouted, "Why don't you answer me? Do you still have the amber?"

The cat was so frustrated, it shouted, "Of course, I still have it!" And of course, the amber fell into the water.

The dog was so angry he shook the cat off his back. Miraculously, the cat made it to shore. But the dog chased it until it finally escaped by climbing a tree.

The dog returned to the river and swam to the spot where the cat dropped the amber. But the water was too deep and murky for him to see the bottom. Then he walked up and down the bank where there were a number of men fishing. Suddenly he caught a whiff of the amber. The smell was coming from a fish one of the fishermen had just pulled in. Quickly he grabbed it with his teeth and raced away before the fisherman could catch him. Carefully he carried the fish home to Ku.

"That's a good dog," said Ku, when the dog dropped the

fish at his feet. "We needed something to eat."

"What's this?" he cried when he cut the fish open. "I can't believe it! It's my amber! My amber!" he said jumping for joy. "You found it, Dog! You found it!"

Ku locked the amber in a chest and went out to buy a jug of wine so he could reopen his tavern. When he returned and opened the chest to get the amber he was surprised to find two money pouches instead of one, two jackets instead of one, and two combs instead of one. Everything in the chest had doubled. And thus Ku learned that the secret of the amber was that it doubled everything it touched.

With this knowledge he became richer than he ever dreamed possible. He made sure that the dog was well fed and often wondered what had happened to his other four-footed companion.

As for the dog, he never again killed a rat, but he chased every cat that crossed his path.

The Man in the Moon
Malaysia

There was once a young man called Sandaranbulan who loved all animals and living things. One day as he was walking along he found a swallow that had fallen at the edge of the road. It hopped about, twittering sadly. Pitying the poor bird, Sandaranbulan carefully picked it up and carried it home. He nursed it with tender care, and after a few days the leg was sound again. To show its gratitude the swallow made a bow to Sandaranbulan and flew off, but shortly it came back with a yellow *mantisan* [pumpkin] seed in its beak, which it presented to its benefactor.

The boy planted the seed in the garden. Day by day the plant grew stronger and stronger. Hidden among the leaves grew an enormous yellow pumpkin. When at last it was ripe, Sandaranbulan gathered the fruit and split it open. To his great surprise, a stream of shining gold and glittering silver came flowing out.

The tale of this miraculous occurrence quickly spread throughout the village, and everyone praised the kind-hearted young man. But there was a very mean child in the neighborhood who nearly became ill with envy. His mouth watered at the tale of such riches. He thought he would also rear a little swallow and get the same reward. It would be easy money, he thought. So he knocked down a swallow that was sitting on the roof, and cared for it carefully as Sandaranbulan had done. When the bird was cured it really did bring him a *mantisan* seed, which he planted in an open space in front of the guest house.

How excited he was when a yellow pumpkin grew underneath the leaves! But on opening it, he received a terrible shock. Out stepped a well-dressed old man, with a book in his left hand, and a pen and a box of red ink in his right. He wore a pleasant, smiling expression, and said quietly to the boy, "You wicked child! How could you be so covetous! But since you worship gold so much, you can come along with me." Then he wrote something in the book, took the boy by the hand, and climbed onto the runners of the pumpkin, which suddenly shot up like a ladder into the sky for the two people to climb on. Beneath them the runners dried up as they passed, so that they could go up but not down.

Before long they arrived at the Palace of Boundless Gold in the moon. The roads were made of shimmering jade set in silver and the palaces were gleaming gold and agates. Everything was so bright that one could not keep one's eyes open, and was so vast that one could not see any end. Still more wonderful were the enchanting fairies, who danced to the accompaniment of heavenly music. Their ineffable beauty bewitched the eyes and ears of the boy, who forgot where he was. After he had looked around for a while, he asked the old man to take him back again. "You want to return, do you?" asked the old man. "Very well. If you can cut down this cinnamon tree here, you can return home; otherwise you cannot." Bringing a silver axe, he handed it to the boy.

In great excitement the boy rushed off with the axe to look at the cinnamon tree, which was made of solid gold with branches festooned with precious stones and agates. He thought to himself, "If I cut down this tree I can take it home, and I won't need to work for the rest of my life." He raised his axe and cut a large notch in the trunk, but as he did so he felt a sharp pain in his shoulders.

Looking around he saw that he had been attacked by a golden eagle. In a rage he drove it away, but when he looked at the tree there was no sign of the blow he had given it. He gave it another slash, and again the eagle struck him. He drove it away again, and once more the cut he had made was not to be seen.

And so it went on and on. He remains there to this day, because the tree never receives more than a single cut before it grows back together again.

If you look up at the moon on a clear night, you can dimly see many trees and people; they are the ones that were in our story of the naughty boy in the Palace of Boundless Gold.

The Story of Tam and Cam
Vietnam

Once upon a time there lived a man, his wife, and their little daughter, Tam. They were good people and lived a happy life until the wife died. After several years, he married again, but the second wife was a wicked woman.

On the first day after the wedding, when there was a big banquet in the house, little Tam was shut up in a room, instead of being allowed to help welcome the guests and attend the feast. Moreover, she was sent to bed without any supper.

Things grew worse when a new baby girl was born. The new child was named Cam, and it was adored by both parents. Poor Tam was now in a worse situation than before, and the stepmother told her husband so many lies about her that he refused to have anything to do with his own daughter.

"Stay in the kitchen and do not annoy us, you naughty child," the wicked stepmother would say.

She gave the little girl a dirty wretched place in the kitchen, and it was there that she had to live and work. At night she slept on a torn mat and had only a ragged sheet as coverlet. Tam was forced to scrub the floors, cut the wood, feed the animals, and do the cooking, washing, and many other tasks. Large blisters formed on her soft little hands, but she bore the pain without complaint. Her stepmother would often send her into the deep forest to gather wood in the secret hope that some wild beast would carry her off. She asked Tam to draw water from wells which were dangerously deep, hoping that she would fall in and drown.

Tam worked so hard that her skin became darkened with dirt and grease, and her hair became matted and scraggly. Whenever she went to the well to draw water, she would look at her image and it frightened her to realize how dirty and ugly she had become. She took some water in the palm of her hand, washed her face, combed her long, smooth hair with her fingers, and the soft white skin appeared again.

When the evil stepmother realized how pretty Tam could look, she hated her more than ever and wished to do her more harm. One day she told Tam and her own daughter, Cam, to go fishing in the village pond.

"Try to catch a lot of fish," she said. "If you come back with only a few, you will be whipped, and sent to bed without your supper."

Tam knew that these words were meant for her, for the stepmother would never think of beating Cam, who was the apple of her eye. But Tam was now used to hard whippings.

Tam fished diligently, and by the end of the day she had a basketful of fish. On the other hand, Cam spent the day rolling in the tender grass, picking wild flowers, basking in the sun, and dancing and singing. The sun had set before Cam even began to fish. She looked at Tam's full basket and then at her own, which was empty. An idea came to her.

"Sister, sister," she cried, "your hair is full of mud. Why don't you wade into the fresh water and wash your hair. Otherwise, mother is going to scold you."

Tam listened to this advice, and swam out into the water to wash her hair. Meanwhile Cam emptied Tam's fish into her own basket, and ran home.

When Tam returned to the shore and realized that her fish had been stolen, her heart sank, and she began to cry bitterly. She was certain her stepmother would punish her severely.

Suddenly a fresh and balmy wind arose, the sky became clear and the clouds whiter, and she saw in front of her the smiling, blue-robed Goddess of Mercy, carrying a green willow branch.

"What is the matter, dear child?" the Goddess asked in a sweet, pure voice.

Tam related all that had happened and added: "Most noble lady, what am I to do tonight when I return home? I am very frightened, for my stepmother will not believe that the fish were stolen. She will whip me very, very hard."

The Goddess of Mercy consoled her. "Your misfortunes will soon be over. Have confidence in me and be of good cheer. Now look in your basket to see whether there is anything left."

Tam looked in the basket and saw a lovely little fish with red fins and golden eyes. She uttered a cry of surprise.

The Goddess told her to take the fish home, put it in the well at the rear of the house, and feed it three times a day with what she could save from her own food.

Tam thanked the Goddess gratefully and did exactly as she had been told. Whenever she went to the well, the fish would appear on the surface to greet her, but never showed itself to anyone else.

The stepmother noticed Tam's strange actions and began to spy on her. She went to the well to look for the fish, but it was hidden in deep water. She then plotted against Tam. One day she ordered her to go to a distant spring to fetch water, and taking advantage of her absence, disguised herself in Tam's ragged clothes and went to the well. She called the fish, and when it came to the surface, scooped it up with a net, and ate it for supper.

When Tam returned home, she went at once to the well and called and called, but the golden fish did not appear. Then she noticed that the surface of the water was stained with blood and realized the truth. Tam leaned her head against the well and wept miserably.

The Goddess of Mercy appeared to her again, and with a face as sweet as that of a loving and compassionate mother, she comforted the child.

"Do not cry," she said. "Your stepmother has killed the fish and eaten it, but you must find the bones and bury them in the ground under your mat. Pray to them and whatever you may wish for will be granted." Tam followed the Goddess's instructions and began to search for the fish's bones, but could find no trace.

"Cluck! Cluck!" said a hen. "Give me some rice, and I will show you where the bones are hidden."

Tam gave her a handful of rice and the hen said, "Cluck! Cluck! Follow me."

When she came to the poultry yard, the hen scratched in a dunghill and uncovered the fish's bones. Tam gathered them up and reburied them as she had been told. It was not long before she received gold and jewelry, and dresses of such wonderful materials they would have rejoiced the heart of any young girl.

Soon it came time for the Autumn Festival, but Tam was ordered to stay at home and sort out two big baskets of black and green beans that the wicked stepmother had purposely mixed together.

"When you have finished your work," she said, "you may go the the festival, but not before."

Then the stepmother and Cam put on their most beautiful dresses and went out. When they had been gone for some time, Tam lifted her tearful face to heaven and prayed, "O benevolent Goddess of Mercy, please help me."

The soft-eyed Goddess appeared at once. With her magic green willow branch, she turned the little flies into sparrows, which sorted the beans for the girl. Tam dried her tears, dressed herself in a glittering, blue-and-silver gown, and went to the festival.

Cam was greatly surprised to see her half-sister at the festival, and whispered to her mother, "That rich lady is strangely like my sister Tam!"

When Tam realized that her stepmother and Cam were

staring at her, she ran away in such a hurry she lost one of her fine slippers.

A court noble discovered the slipper and presented it to the king.

The king examined the slipper carefully and declared he had never before seen such a work of art. He asked the ladies of the court to try it on, but the slipper was too small for even the smallest foot among the noble ladies. Then he sent messengers throughout the kingdom with orders for all women everywhere to try on the slipper; but it would fit none of them. Finally, word was sent out that the woman whose foot could fit the slipper would become his queen.

At last, it was Tam's turn to try the slipper. It fitted her foot perfectly. She then appeared in court wearing both slippers and her glittering blue-and-silver gown, looking extremely beautiful. She was married to the king at a big wedding attended by many dignitaries, and thenceforth led a brilliant and happy life.

All this was too much for the stepmother and Cam to accept. They could not bear to see Tam so happy and they would have killed her willingly. But owing to the king's protection they were afraid.

On her father's name's day, Tam returned home to celebrate with her family. At that time, however great and important one might be, one was always expected by one's parents to behave exactly like a young and obedient child. The cunning stepmother took advantage of this custom, and asked Tam to climb an areca tree to obtain some nuts for the guests. As Tam was queen, she could have refused, but she was a very pious and dutiful daughter, so climbed the tree. While there, she felt it swaying to and fro in a strange and alarming manner.

"What are you doing?" she asked her stepmother.

"I am only trying to frighten the ants, which might bite you, my dear child," came the reply.

But in fact, the wicked stepmother had obtained an axe, and she cut down the tree, which fell with a crash. Poor Tam was killed instantly.

"Now we are rid of her," said the horrid woman, with an ugly laugh. "She will never come back. We shall report to the king that she died in an accident, and my beloved daughter, Cam, will become queen in her stead!"

Things happened exactly as she had planned, and Cam became the king's wife.

But Tam's pure and innocent soul could find no rest. She was turned into a nightingale, living in a beautiful grove near the king's garden.

One day, one of the palace maids was airing the king's dragon-embroidered robe, and the nightingale sang in her melodious voice, "O sweet maid, be careful with my husband's robe and do not tear it by putting it on a thorny hedge."

The nightingale sang so sweetly she moved the hearts of all who heard her. Even the king was attracted by her voice. She sang so sadly that tears came into his eyes. At last the king said, "Delightful nightingale, if you are the soul of my beloved queen, be pleased to settle in my wide sleeves."

The gentle bird went straight into the king's sleeves, and rubbed her smooth head against his hand.

She was then put in a golden cage in the king's bedroom. The king became so fond of her that he would stay near the cage all day listening to her beautiful melancholic songs.

Cam became jealous of the nightingale and sought her mother's advice. One day, while the king was holding a council with his ministers, Cam killed the bird, and threw the feathers into the royal gardens.

"What is the meaning of this?" asked the king, when he saw the empty cage.

There was great confusion in the palace. Everyone looked for the nightingale, but no one could find it.

151

"Perhaps she was bored and flew off," said Cam.

The king was very sad, but there was nothing he could do about it, other than resign himself to fate.

Once again, however, Tam's restless soul was transformed. This time it became a great, magnificent tree. It bore only a single fruit, but what a wonderful fruit it was! It was perfectly round, large, and had a very sweet smell. An old woman passing by the tree and seeing the beautiful fruit said,

> Golden fruit, golden fruit,
> Drop into the bag of this old woman.
> This one will never eat you.
> She will keep you and enjoy your beauty.

The fruit at once dropped into the old woman's bag. She took it home to enjoy its appearance and fragrant smell. But the next day, on returning from some errands, to her great surprise she found her house clean and tidy, and a delicious hot meal waiting for her. It was as if some magic hand had done this during her absence.

The following morning the old woman pretended to go out, but she returned stealthily, and watched the house. Soon she beheld a fair and slender lady coming out of the golden fruit. She was even more surprised when the lady began to tidy up the house. The old woman rushed into the room and tore away the peel, so that the fair lady could no longer hide herself within the fruit. The young lady then had to remain in the house and consider the old woman as her mother.

One day the king went hunting and became lost. He saw the old woman's house and asked for shelter. According to custom, the latter offered him some tea and betel. The king observed the delicate way in which the betel had been prepared and asked, "Who made this betel? It looks exactly like that prepared by my late beloved queen."

In a trembling voice, the old woman replied, "Son of Heaven, it was made by my unworthy daughter."

The king then ordered the daughter to be brought before him. When she came in, she bowed low, and he immediately realized that it was Tam, his beloved queen. They both wept bitter tears after such a long separation and so much unhappiness. Tam then returned to the capital with the king, where she took her rightful place as first wife and queen.

Cam was completely forgotten by the king.

She then thought to herself, "If I were as beautiful as my sister, I would win the king's heart." She asked the queen, "Dearest sister, how can my skin become as white as yours?"

"It is very simple," answered the queen who was now completely aware of Cam's ill will. "You have only to jump into a vat of boiling water."

Cam believed her and did as she was told.

This was the end of Cam, and she died instantly.

When the wicked stepmother learned of Cam's death, she wept so long that she became blind, and shortly after, died of a broken heart.

Queen Tam was now free of her enemies, and lived the rest of her life in peace and happiness.

Ghosts,
Dreams, and
The Supernatural

Fear of the unknown is one of the most powerful of human emotions. One way to make the unknown known, and thus less terrifying, is to name it, give it shape, and make stories about it. Where European people have ghosts and giants, leprechauns, trolls, and poltergeists to explain unexpected accidents or bad luck, Asian cultures have their own sets of supernatural beings, including the Japanese *oni* (evil ogres) and Korean *tokkaebi* (mischievous gremlins), as well as a wide variety of ghosts, demons, gods, and spirits, both good and evil. If even women and children can escape from ogres in stories, perhaps anyone can hope to escape from the powerful forces they fear.

In Asian cultures animals are commonly ascribed supernatural powers, especially the power to assume human form. Supernatural animals sometimes help people who have helped them; stories of such events are very much like the stories of Magic Gifts. On the other hand, animal or other spirits may take the form of beautiful women or handsome men and seduce vulnerable human beings, eventually causing their death. Stories such as "The Painted Skin" and "The Pedlar's Son" are cautionary tales warning of that most alluring danger which many are too foolish to fear—physical lust.

Dreams connect mundane human life with the supernatural world. In a dream one's spirit leaves the body and may travel in time and space to visit people who have died, or who live far away. Supernatural beings often choose dreams as the medium through which to speak to people, to show them the future, or to help them confront truths not apparent in waking life.

The *Oni's* Laughter
Japan

Long ago in a certain place there was a wealthy man with an only daughter who was very beautiful. It was decided that she should be married to a young man in a distant village. When the day for the marriage came, a splendid palanquin arrived from the bridegroom's village to carry the bride to her new home. The girl's mother and a great crowd of her relatives followed along after the palanquin calling, "The bride! The bride!" as they crossed over the mountains and mountain passes. As they were going along a black cloud suddenly came from out of the sky and enveloped the bride's palanquin. When they saw this they began crying, "What shall we do? What shall we do?" But the black cloud snatched the bride from the palanquin, flew away with her, and disappeared.

The mother nearly became insane with worry about her daughter. "I must go and find her, no matter what happens," she said. Putting some cooked food in a pack on her back she set off, searching aimlessly about in the mountains.

She crossed fields and mountains, always searching and searching. Finally the sun began to set. Just then she saw a tiny temple in the distance. She went up to it and called, "I know that I look terrible, but could you please let me stay here, just for tonight." A priestess came from the temple and said, "I have nothing for you to sleep in and nothing for you to eat, but nevertheless you are welcome to stay." The mother entered the temple, and since she was so tired, she soon lay down to sleep.

The priestess took off her own robe and spread it over the woman. Then she said, "Your daughter for whom you are searching is being held in the *oni*'s mansion over across the river. There is a big dog and a little dog guarding there, so you cannot get across. Still, during the middle of the day, they sometimes take a nap, so you might be able to get across then. However, the bridge is an abacus bridge, and since there are many beads on it, you must be very careful how you step on it. If you miss one of the beads, you will fall through to the village of your birth; so do be careful."

The next morning the mother, surprised by a rustling noise, *sawa sawa,* suddenly woke up. There she found herself on a plain where reeds grew profusely. Neither the temple nor the priestess were to be seen. There were only the reeds moaning, *sawa sawa,* in the morning wind. The mother saw that she had been sleeping exposed to the wind and rain with only a stone monument for a pillow. "Thank you, priestess," she said, and set off for the river bank as she had been told.

Just at that time the large dog and the small dog were taking a nap. Seeing that this was her chance, she carefully walked over the abacus bridge. Having crossed safely over the river, she went on and soon heard the familiar sound, *chan chan, chan karin,* of someone using a loom. Without thinking, the mother called, "Daughter!" The girl looked out the door; then the two of them ran and joyously embraced each other. The girl hurriedly cooked her mother some supper; then she said, "It will be too bad for you if the *oni* finds you here," and she hid her in a stone chest.

Soon the *oni* came home. "It seems to me that it smells as if human beings are here," he said, sniffing, *kun kun,* with his nose. The girl said that she knew nothing about it, but the *oni* said, "If I look at the flower in the garden, I can tell."

Now there was a magical flower in the garden which always had just as many blossoms on it as there were human beings in the house. On this day there were three flowers in bloom, and the *oni* came back into the house in a great rage. "Where do you have those humans hidden?" he demanded, looking as if he were going to attack her at any moment. The girl wondered what she could possibly do.

Suddenly an idea came to her. "I have become pregnant; perhaps that is why there are three flowers."

When he heard that, the *oni,* who had been so angry, suddenly was so overjoyed that he nearly stood on his head. In his joy he shouted to assemble his retainers saying, "Retainers, bring *sake* [rice wine] and drums; go and kill the dogs guarding the river!" And he danced around for joy. The retainers, too, were delighted and began shouting noisily: "Get the *sake,* get the drums! Kill the big dog, kill the little dog!"

Finally all the *oni* became drunk on the *sake* and fell asleep. The *oni* general said, "Wife, I'm sleepy, show me where my wooden box is." The girl, upon hearing that he wanted his wooden box, was greatly relieved. She helped him get in it, then closed its seven lids and locked its seven locks. Hurriedly she got her mother from the stone box, and they fled from the *oni*'s house.

Since the large dog and the small dog had been killed, there was nothing to worry about there, so they went to the storehouse where the vehicles were kept. "Shall we take a ten-thousand-*ri* chariot or a thousand-*ri* chariot?" they asked one another, but just then the priestess came and said: "Neither the ten-thousand-*ri* chariot nor the thousand-*ri* chariot will be any good. You should escape in the swift ship." The mother and her daughter got in the ship and fled away on the river as fast as they could.

The *oni,* asleep in the wooden box, became thirsty and called, "Wife, bring me some water," but no matter how many times he called, there was no answer. He broke the seven lids off the box, got out and looked around, but the girl was not there. No matter where he looked, there was no trace of her at all. "Did that slut get away?" he cried. He jerked his retainers awake, and they went to the vehicle storehouse. They saw that the ship was gone, so they all went down to the river. There they could see the mother and her daughter just disappearing in the distance.

"Drink up all the water in the river!" commanded the *oni* general, and the whole crowd of *oni* immediately dropped down, stuck their heads in the water and *gabu gabu,* began drinking it up. Soon the water in the river began to fall, and the ship in which the mother and daughter were fleeing began to float back to where the *oni* were. It looked as though the *oni* would be able to reach out and grab them at any moment. The mother and daughter had already given up any hope of being saved, when just then the priestess appeared again. "Why are you here just doing nothing?" she asked. "Hurry, show your 'important place' to the *oni!*"

The priestess joined them, and all three of them began rolling up their kimonos. When the *oni* saw that, they began to roar with laughter, *gera gera.* They rolled over and

161

over in laughter and when they did that, all the water which they had drunk came up again and so the ship sailed off into the distance. In this way the mother and her daughter were saved from danger.

They thanked the priestess again and again, saying that this was all because of her help. The priestess said, "I am actually a stone monument. Every year please erect another monument beside me; that is what I will enjoy more than anything else." Then she disappeared from sight.

The mother and daughter were able to return home safely, and they never forgot their obligation to the priestess; every year they erected another stone monument for her.

The Vampire Cat
Japan

The Prince of Hizen, a distinguished member of the Nabeshima family, lingered in the garden with O Toyo, the favorite among his ladies. When the sun set they retired to the palace, but failed to notice that they were being followed by a large cat.

O Toyo went to her room and fell asleep. At midnight she awoke and gazed about her, as if suddenly aware of some dreadful presence in the apartment. At length she saw, crouching close beside her, a gigantic cat, and before she could cry out for assistance the animal sprang upon her and strangled her. The animal then made a hole under the veranda, buried the corpse, and assumed the form of the beautiful O Toyo.

The prince, who knew nothing of what had happened,

continued to love the false O Toyo, unaware that in reality he was caressing a foul beast. He noticed, little by little, that his strength failed, and it was not long before he became dangerously ill. Physicians were summoned, but they could do nothing to restore the royal patient. It was observed that he suffered most during the night, and was troubled by horrible dreams. This being so his councillors arranged that a hundred retainers should sit with their lord and keep watch while he slept.

The watch went into the sickroom, but just before ten o'-clock it was overcome by a mysterious drowsiness. When all the men were asleep the false O Toyo crept into the apartment and disturbed the prince until sunrise. Night after night the retainers came to guard their master, but always they fell asleep at the same hour, and even three loyal councillors had a similar experience.

During this time the prince grew worse, and at length a priest named Ruiten was appointed to pray on his behalf. One night, while he was engaged in his supplications, he heard a strange noise proceeding from the garden. On looking out of the window he saw a young soldier washing himself. When he had finished his ablutions he stood before an image of Buddha, and prayed most ardently for the recovery of the prince.

Ruiten, delighted to find such zeal and loyalty, invited the young man to enter his house, and when he had done so inquired his name.

"I am Ito Soda," said the young man, "and serve in the infantry of Nabeshima. I have heard of my lord's sickness and long to have the honor of nursing him; but being of low rank it is not meet that I should come into his presence. I have, nevertheless, prayed to the Buddha that my lord's life may be spared. I believe that the Prince of Hizen is bewitched, and if I might remain with him I would do my utmost to find and crush the evil power that is the cause of his illness."

Ruiten was so favorably impressed with these words that he went the next day to consult with one of the councillors, and after much discussion it was arranged that Ito Soda should keep watch with the hundred retainers.

When Ito Soda entered the royal apartment he saw that his master slept in the middle of the room, and he also observed the hundred retainers sitting in the chamber quietly chatting together in the hope that they would be able to keep off approaching drowsiness. By ten o'clock all the retainers, in spite of their efforts, had fallen asleep. Ito Soda tried to keep his eyes open, but a heaviness was gradually overcoming him, and he realized that if he wished to keep awake he must resort to extreme measures. When he had carefully spread oil paper over the mats he stuck his dirk into his thigh. The sharp pain he experienced warded off sleep for a time, but eventually he felt his eyes closing once more. Resolved to outwit the spell which had proved too much for the retainers, he twisted the knife in his thigh, and thus increased the pain and kept his loyal watch, while blood continually dripped upon the oil paper.

While Ito Soda watched he saw the sliding doors drawn open and a beautiful woman creep softly into the apartment. With a smile she noticed the sleeping retainers, and was about to approach the prince when she observed Ito Soda. After she had spoken curtly to him she approached the prince and inquired how he fared, but the prince was too ill to make a reply.

Ito Soda watched every movement. The woman tried to bewitch the prince, but she was always frustrated in her evil purpose by the dauntless eyes of Ito Soda, and at last was compelled to retire.

In the morning the retainers awoke, and were filled with shame when they learnt how Ito Soda had kept his vigil. The councillors loudly praised the young soldier for his loyalty and enterprise, and he was commanded to keep watch again that night.

He did so, and once more the false O Toyo entered the sickroom, and, as on the previous night, she was compelled to retreat without being able to cast her spell over the prince.

It was discovered that since the faithful Soda had kept guard, the prince was able to obtain peaceful slumber, and, moreover, that he began to get better; for the false O Toyo, having been frustrated on two occasions, now kept away altogether, and the guard was not troubled with mysterious drowsiness. Soda, impressed by these strange circumstances, went to one of the councillors and informed him that the so-called O Toyo was a goblin of some kind.

That night Soda planned to go to the creature's room and try to kill her, arranging that in case she should escape there should be eight retainers outside waiting to capture her and dispatch her immediately.

At the appointed hour Soda went to the creature's apartment, pretending that he bore a message from the prince.

"What is your message?" inquired the woman.

"Kindly read this letter," replied Soda, and with these words he drew his dirk and tried to kill her.

The false O Toyo seized a halberd and endeavored to strike her adversary. Blow followed blow, but at last perceiving that flight would serve her better than battle she threw away her weapon, and in a moment the lovely maiden turned into a cat and sprang onto the roof. The eight men waiting outside in case of emergency shot at the animal, but the creature succeeded in eluding them.

The cat made all speed for the mountains, and caused trouble among the people who lived in the vicinity, but was finally killed during a hunt ordered by the Prince of Hizen. The prince became well again, and Ito Soda received the honor and reward he so richly deserved.

The Painted Skin
China

In the city of Taiyuan there lived a scholar named Wang. One morning when he was out for an early stroll he saw a woman walking slowly down the road, carrying a cloth bundle over her shoulder. Wang quickened his pace and caught up with her, and he saw that she was a beautiful young woman, about eighteen years of age.

He asked her, "Why are you out all alone so early in the morning?" She replied, "What's the point of asking? There's nothing you can do to help me in my distress." "What distress?" he asked. "Perhaps I could help you if you would tell me what is wrong."

The woman replied sadly, "My parents, out of greed, sold me to a wealthy household as a concubine. The first wife is jealous. She scolds me and beats me, morning, noon, and night, until I can bear it no longer. I am running away."

"Where will you go?" asked Wang. "I do not know," she replied. "I shall go where my fate takes me." "My house is not far from here. Why don't you come with me?" said the scholar.

The young woman agreed, and Wang, taking her bundle, led her to his house. Seeing that there was no one in the room the young woman said, "Have you no family?" "This is my study," he replied. "The place suits me quite well," she said, "but please do not tell anyone that I am here." Wang agreed, and spent the night with her, and for several days no one knew of her presence.

Wang did, however, tell his wife. She wanted to send the woman away, thinking she might be a runaway maid from a wealthy family, but Wang refused to let her do so.

One day when Wang was in the marketplace a Daoist priest caught sight of him and said with alarm, "What has happened to you?" "Nothing," he replied. "There is something unsettled about your demeanor," the priest continued, "How can you say nothing has happened?" The scholar continued to deny that anything unusual had taken place. The priest then departed, saying, "How foolish! There are people who don't even know when they are about to die!"

The scholar thought this was a strange remark, and began to wonder if the priest could be warning him about the young woman. But then he recalled how beautiful she was—surely she could not be an evil spirit, and he began to suspect that the Daoist was simply trying to drum up business.

When he got home he found that the gate had been barred from within, and he could not enter. Puzzled, he clambered through a hole in the wall, only to find that the door of his study was also locked. He tiptoed up to the window, and looking in he saw a hideous demon, dark green in color, with pointed teeth, spreading a human skin on the mat and painting on it with colored brushes.

Then the demon put down the brushes and shook out the skin, like a piece of clothing, then put it on and was transformed into the beautiful young woman.

The scholar was terrified by what he saw, and he crept away from the window and fled from the house. He tried to find the Daoist priest, but the priest was not to be found in the marketplace.

After much searching he found him outside the city. Wang knelt at the priest's feet and begged for help. The priest said, "Please let the demon go. This creature is also suffering. It has only now found a body in which to dwell, and I do not wish to harm it."

Then he gave the scholar a magic fly whisk and instructed him to hang it over the door outside his bedroom. As he took his leave, he promised to meet the scholar again at Green Emperor Temple.

The scholar returned home and dared not enter his study, but went straight to his bedroom and hung the fly whisk above the door. Just after dark he heard a rustling sound. He was afraid to look for himself, so he asked his wife to go see what it was. He wife reported that she had seen the woman come to their door but hesitate on seeing the fly whisk. The woman had stood there a long while, grinding her teeth, and then left.

A short time later she returned, cursing, "Why should I fear the Daoist's hex? Should I spit out what I've only now begun to savor?"

Then she smashed the fly whisk, broke down the bedroom door and rushed headlong into the room. She went straight to the bed and ripped open the scholar's chest, pulled out his heart, and fled. His wife called out for the maid, who brought in a lamp, but when they looked they saw that Wang was dead, his chest bloody and mangled. His wife wept silently, afraid to make a sound.

The next day Wang's wife sent his younger brother to find the Daoist priest. The priest said angrily, "I took pity on the demon, and see how it has paid me back!" Then he went with Wang's brother to look for the woman, but she was nowhere to be seen.

After a moment the priest raised his head, gazed in the four directions, and said, "She has not gone far." Then he asked, "Who lives in the southern garden?" "I do," said the brother. "That's where she is," said the priest. The brother could not believe it. The priest asked, "Have any strangers come by here today?" "I was at Green Emperor Temple looking for you, so I don't know," said the brother, "but I will ask the others." Soon he returned and said, "As it happens, an old woman came early this morning, looking for work as a maid. She is still here." The Daoist said, "She is the one."

So they went together to find the old woman. The Daoist priest pointed his magic peach-wood sword at her and shouted, "Vile demon! Return my whisk!" The old woman trembled and grew pale, and tried to flee. The Daoist priest blocked her way, she fell with a thud, and her skin split open revealing an ugly demon who writhed on the ground grunting like a pig. The Daoist chopped off its head with his peach-wood sword, and its body turned into thick smoke which lay piled in coils just above the ground.

The priest then pulled out a bottle-gourd, removed its stopper, and drew the smoke into it, just as a person draws a deep breath. When all the smoke was in the bottle the priest replaced the stopper and put the bottle in his pouch. Then they all looked at the painted skin, which was perfect in every detail from head to toe. The priest rolled it up, as one would roll a painted scroll, putting it too in his pouch.

He was about to leave when Wang's wife approached him, weeping, and begged him to return her husband to life. The Daoist declined, saying that he had no such power. The woman grew more and more distraught, and threw herself on the ground, refusing to get up. The Daoist thought for a moment and said, "My skills are limited, and I truly am not able to bring him back to life. But I know someone who might be able to help you. It won't hurt to go ask him." "Who is it?" she asked. "In the marketplace," he replied, "there is a madman who often sleeps on the dungheap. You can ask him to help you. But do not allow yourself to become angry if he treats you rudely." Wang's brother knew of this man, and taking leave of the Daoist, he went with Wang's wife to look for him.

When they got to the marketplace they saw a beggar in the street, singing some incomprehensible song. Long strands of snot hung from his nose, and he was so filthy one could hardly bear to be near him. Wang's wife approached him on her knees. The beggar laughed and said, "Have you fallen for me?" Wang's wife told him her request. He laughed again and said, "The world is full of men, why do you want him back?" She persisted. Then he said, "Strange! A man dies and you ask me to bring him back to life. Am I Yama, King of the Underworld?" Angrily he struck her with his staff. She bore the blow without complaint, as crowds gathered to watch. Then the beggar took a handful of snot and spittle and thrust it at Wang's wife, saying, "Eat this!" Her face turned bright crimson, and she was filled with revulsion, but then she remembered the Daoist priest's instructions and forced herself to swallow it. When it entered her throat it felt hard like a knot, but she forced it down, and it stopped in her chest.

The beggar laughed and said, "You *have* fallen for me!" Then he walked away, not looking back. She followed him into a temple, hoping to press him further, but he had disappeared, and though she looked everywhere, not a trace of him was to be found. There was nothing she could do but return home. Grief-stricken at her husband's death, humiliated by having eaten the spittle, she wept bitterly and wanted only to die.

She went to prepare the corpse, which the servants were afraid to touch. As she was at this task, weeping, she felt a lump in her gullet, and had an urge to vomit. Suddenly the lump emerged from her mouth and fell into his chest. Startled, she looked at it, and saw it was a human heart. It began to move about in his chest, and a warm vapor puffed out from it like smoke. She was amazed and held the wound tightly closed with her hands, but the vapor continued to emerge from the seam of the wound. Then she tore a piece of cloth and bound the wound. As she lifted the corpse she noticed that it was gradually growing warmer, so she covered him with a fur coverlet.

That night he began to breathe, and the next day he was alive again. He said, "I feel confused, as in a dream, and there is a pain in my chest." A small scar was visible on his chest, about the size of a coin, which gradually disappeared.

Storyteller's comment: "How foolish was this man! What clearly was a demon, he considered a beauty. How muddled was this foolish man! What clearly was a true warning, he considered false. He loved beauty and chased after it, and his wife had to eat spittle. 'Heaven's Way is to Repay,' but the the foolish never learn. Alas!"

The Man Who Sold a Ghost
China

In the city of Nanyang there lived a man named Song Dingbo, who was both brave and clever. One evening he set off on a journey to the neighboring city of Wancheng. As he left the city gates, night was already falling, and when he got as far as the graveyard a few miles away, he could hardly see the road in front of him.

Suddenly he heard a rustling sound, and a strange figure, not quite human, appeared before him. "Who are you, sir?" Song Dingbo asked.

"I am a ghost. Who are you?" the other replied in a small voice.

When Song Dingbo heard this he did not know what to do. The last thing he had expected was to encounter a ghost, and a timid one at that! He decided to play a trick on the apparition, so he said, "I am a ghost, too!"

"Oh, that's good. Otherwise I would have to frighten you," said the ghost, breathing a sigh of relief. "Where are you going?" he added.

Song Dingbo did not want to reveal that he was going to Wancheng, so he simply said, "I'm going east."

"East? That means you are probably headed for Wancheng, which is where I'm going too," said the ghost.

"All right, let's go together. After all, two people traveling together are safer than one alone," Song Dingbo replied.

"Not *people—ghosts!*" his companion corrected him.

"Yes, of course, *ghosts!*" said Song Dingbo.

The two of them walked and talked, talked and walked, and after a while the ghost said, "I'm getting tired of walking. Why don't we take turns carrying each other, and that way one can rest while the other one walks."

"Fine. I'll carry you first," said Song Dingbo, hoisting the ghost onto his shoulders. He was surprised at how light the ghost was, almost as if he had no weight at all.

Soon it was time to switch places. Song Dingbo carefully climbed onto the ghost's shoulders, but the ghost exclaimed, "How strange! You are awfully clumsy for a ghost, and you weigh almost as much as a living person!"

Song Dingbo replied, "That's because I haven't been dead very long. Please forgive me!"

"Oh, so that's it," said the ghost, panting and struggling under his burden.

"Since I am new at being a ghost, perhaps you could give me a few tips," said Song Dingbo. "Like, what should we fear most of all?"

"You mean you don't even know *that?* You really are not quite all here," said the ghost. "The first thing to watch out for is human spit. If the spit of a living person gets on you, you won't be able to change your form."

"Aha!" Song Dingbo said to himself. "He has revealed

his secret! When morning comes, and he has to hide his ghostly form, I will take care of him!"

As it was almost dawn, Song Dingbo said to the ghost, "You have carried me long enough. Now it's my turn to carry you."

Once again he hoisted the ghost onto his shoulders, taking care to hold him tight. The ghost could tell that something was amiss, and when he realized that his companion was a man and not a ghost, he began to wail and squirm. But Song Dingbo held him tightly and would not let go, all the while walking as fast as he could go toward Wancheng.

When they reached the city the sky was already growing light. Song Dingbo threw the ghost down, and the ghost rolled along the ground and turned into a sheep, trying to run away. But Song Dingbo remembered the secret he had learned. He grabbed the sheep by its horns, spat on it, tied a rope around its neck, and led it down the street toward the marketplace. Not long after, a merchant offered to buy the sheep for a thousand coppers. And that's how Song Dingbo sold a ghost.

The Legend of Arang
Korea

On the high bank of the river Nagdong in the district of Miryang, in the province of south Gyongsang, there stands a lofty tower, called Yongnam-Nu. Just below this tower along the steep cliffs that border the river there is a dense grove of bamboos. In this grove there once stood a small memorial shrine, but today nothing remains but a tiny stone monument to commemorate the sad story of the virgin named Arang.

Her surname was Yun, and her personal name in childhood Zong-Og, or "Chaste Jade." Her father was a nobleman of Seoul who was appointed magistrate in Miryang, where these sad events took place. She came there with her father when she was eighteen years of age. She was very pretty, and advanced in the study of the classics, so that many suitors came to woo her. In her father's opinion, however, none of them was a suitable match for her, and she remained unmarried.

Among the officials of low rank there was a young bachelor named Beg Ga, whose duty it was to carry the magistrate's seal. Attracted by the beauty of the magistrate's daughter he devised a plan to win her love, for humble man as he was he could not speak directly to her, and marriage with her was out of the question. He therefore became friendly with her nurse and disclosed his secret to her.

One evening when Arang was reading in her room her nurse came to her and said with a smile, "Tonight the moon is full. Wouldn't you like to go for a stroll outside? The view from the tower of the river and the wide expanse of reeds would be delightful. Come with me and see it."

Arang went out into the garden with her nurse. They stood for a while by the lotus pond admiring the pale moonlight shining through the stillness of the night. Anxious not to be too long because she had not asked her father's permission to go out, Arang said, "It is very late, Nurse, I must be going back." But her nurse paid no attention to her and insisted that she come and see the view from the Yongnam tower. Somewhat reluctantly Arang followed her to the top of the tower. There she sat on the balcony and looked down on the beauty of the night.

The young official Beg was already hiding behind one of the thick wooden pillars awaiting her arrival. The nurse now made some excuse to leave the lady, and as soon as she had gone the young man stepped out and whispered to Arang, "Do not be afraid. You do not know me, but I love you to distraction." Arang was terrified at this unexpected intrusion, and screaming loudly tried to run away.

But there was no one there except the young man who rushed at her and tried to take her in his arms. She resisted strongly, and the young man drew his dagger to threaten her. Arang resisted him to the last, when he stabbed her and she fell dead on the floor. Her body he threw into the bamboo grove below the tower.

Next morning, when it was discovered that Arang was missing, her father ordered the most careful investigation. Not the slightest clue could be found, for the nurse and the young official Beg contrived to keep their connection with the affair quite secret. Because of the shame of this incident, which should not have happened in a noble family, the magistrate himself resigned and returned to Seoul.

Thereafter, when any new magistrate took up his post in Miryang he was found dead the very next morning. There was never any trace of his having been murdered, however, and the mysterious death of every new magistrate on the night of his arrival greatly perplexed the Government in Seoul. Thenceforth no one was willing to be appointed magistrate of Miryang.

One day an official named Yi Sang-Sa applied for this post, for he had in mind a scheme to clear up the mystery of his predecessors' deaths. On being appointed by the Government he came to Miryang. The officials there made preparations for the funeral which they thought would take place on the following morning.

On the night of his arrival the new magistrate Yi lit as many candles as he could to illuminate every corner of his residence, and sitting in the center of the hall began to read in a loud voice. Suddenly a strange wind sprang up, the door opened of its own accord, and there appeared the ghost of a girl, with her hair in disorder, one arm and one breast cut off, and a dagger piercing her throat.

Not in the least horrified by the terrible apparition, the magistrate shouted boldly, "Are you a ghost or a living creature?" The ghost replied, "I am the spirit of Arang lingering in this world because my revenge is not yet accomplished. Whenever I have come to a new magistrate on his first night, he has been horrified by my appearance and has died of fright, but you are the boldest and bravest magistrate I have ever seen. My murderer goes to your office every day. At roll call on the third day from now a yellow moth will flutter round him. By this sign you shall know him and you will be able to punish him on my behalf."

Next morning the officials who had prepared a funeral for the new magistrate were greatly surprised to find him alive. At roll call on the third day he saw a yellow moth flying to and fro over the back of a young official named Beg Ga. He summoned this fellow to appear before him, and confronted with his crime he confessed everything. He was found guilty and executed at once. They found the girl's body in the grove, and buried it where it lay. After this the ghost appeared no more. A shrine was built beside her grave where people came to pray, and even to hold an annual festival to avert calamities and ensure the safety of the town.

The Centipede Girl
Korea

There once was a poor man who lived on the outskirts of Seoul. He was so poor that he could neither provide food for his family, nor keep a roof over their heads. His dire poverty reduced him to the uttermost depths of despair, and at last in the extremity of his misery he resolved to put an end to his life.

One day he left his wife without telling her where he was going. He went down to the banks of the Han River, and walked along until he came to a towering rocky cliff. He climbed to the top, closed his eyes, and hurled himself over the precipice into the deep water below. He imagined that he must be killed instantly. Half an hour later, however, a beautiful woman who was washing clothes by the riverside found him lying on a sandbank. He was unconscious, but otherwise completely unhurt.

Before long he came to his senses, and she asked him what had happened. He told her of his poverty, and his resolve to end his life. So she said to him, "Happily you are safe. I hope you will never try to do such a terrible thing again. You are still young, and sometime Fortune will smile on you. If you like you can come home with me and rest a while at my house."

Thereupon she led him away, and soon they came to her house. It was very large and built of brick, and stood alone in the valley. Altogether it gave an impression of great wealth. The man stayed there as a guest, and very soon fell in love with the girl. He forgot his family completely. In any case he was sure he must be dead, for had he not thrown himself in the river to put an end to his life? Never in his wildest dreams had he imagined that any such delights could exist in the world as the life he was now leading with this mysterious girl. She was of the most ethereal beauty, and gave him the finest clothes to wear, and the richest food to eat. Moreover the house itself was luxurious beyond his wildest imaginings, and he was completely overwhelmed by it all.

They lived together happily for a few months. Then,

however, his new life began to pall a little, and he thought wistfully of his helpless family in Seoul. So he told his mistress that he would like to go away for a while, though he did not tell her that he wanted to visit his family. But she had already guessed his intention, and said, "If you leave me now, I am afraid that you will forget me and never come back."

The man too thought that it was quite possible that he might stay with his family and not return to her, but he answered vehemently, "How could I ever forget you? Have no fear. I will come back to you without fail."

"On your way back, then," said the girl, "take no notice of anyone who may try to deter you. Come straight back, and I shall be waiting for you."

So he left her, and set out for his own house, where he had left his own family. When he reached the village he was astounded to see a magnificent new house built where his old home had stood. When he came closer he saw his own name on the gate. A sudden suspicion flashed into his mind that his wife might have been unfaithful in his absence. This thought made him rather angry, but then he reflected that he had no right to blame her, for he had neglected her for a long time.

He knocked at the gate, and his son came and opened it. He looked at his long-lost father with joyous tears in his eyes. "Welcome home, Father," he cried, and then called to his mother, "Mother, Father is home!" She immediately rushed out into the garden, wearing the most beautiful clothes.

Her husband looked sternly at her and asked, "Who built this house? Where did you get the money?"

His wife looked at him questioningly. "Wasn't it you who sent me money every day? I thought it was you who sent us all these wonderful presents. Am I mistaken, then?"

The truth slowly dawned on her husband. It must have

been none other than the rich woman he had stayed with, for there could be no one else who would help his family. So he pretended he had just been joking, and changed the subject. He said nothing of his suicide, nor of the mysterious woman he had met.

He was very happy to be reunited with his family after his long absence, but as the months went by he began to think longingly of the beautiful woman he had left in the country. At last his desire to see her once again became so strong that he could bear to wait no longer. Once again he left his wife and family and set out for his mistress's house.

On the way he had to pass by a big hollow tree. Just as he came to it he was surprised to hear a voice calling him by name. "My dear grandson," it said, "I am the spirit of your grandfather. Listen to me. You must not visit that woman again. I give you this warning for your own good. She is no woman, but a centipede a thousand years old."

It certainly sounded like his grandfather's voice, but he refused to believe what it had told him, for he trusted the woman implicitly. He would not have been deterred even if the warning had been true, for having once attempted suicide he was no longer afraid of death. So he answered, "Grandfather, I must see her again. I promised her I would return, and nothing will prevent me from keeping my promise. Death is nothing to me, for I believe that I have died once already. And even though it meant death, I would see her, for it was she who saved my family when starvation stared them in the face."

The disembodied voice spoke solemnly to him. "I see that you are determined to go," it said. "There is one way for you to escape death. Go and buy the strongest tobacco you can, smoke it, and keep the juices in your mouth. As soon as you see her, spit them in her face. If you fail to do this you will surely die. Poor man, she has cast a spell on you with her beauty."

So he went to the market and bought the strongest tobacco he could find. Then he set out again, and smoked hard all the way to his mistress's house. He carefully stored the tobacco juices in his mouth. When he got to her house he peeped in through a crack in the gate, and there he saw the tail of a great centipede in the house. Undaunted, he determined to see her once again, whatever the outcome. So he boldly knocked at the door. His mistress came out and opened the gate and received him gladly. But he spoke not a word, for he was still holding the poisonous tobacco juices in his mouth. Seeing his clenched mouth and the strange expression of his eyes, she guessed that something must have happened, and she turned pale in her alarm.

He came into the room and gazed at her. She was as beautiful as ever, just as he remembered her. Her raven hair, her eyes clear as crystal, the curve of her brow, her nose and mouth—all were just as they had been before. He was torn between his love for her and the dire warning his grandfather's spirit had given him. He was on the point of spitting the poisonous tobacco juice in her face, when she suddenly gave a sob. She bowed her head and wept. He stared at her, undecided, and it seemed that she became twice as beautiful as before. As he looked he relented and turning to the window, spat out the tobacco juices.

Her anxiety passed and she smiled. "Thank you for sparing me," she said. "The voice that you heard is not your grandfather's. It was the accursed snake that lives in the hollow tree. I am a daughter of the Heavenly King, and the snake was one of the servants in the palace. He fell in love with me and seduced me. The matter came to the ears of my Heavenly Father and he punished us both. Me, he ordered to live for three years in the world of men as a centipede, and my seducer he condemned to live eternally as a snake. Ever resentful of his fate, he has always tried to do me further harm. Today is the last day of my sentence, and tomorrow I return to my father. Had you spat in my face I should have had to suffer three long years more."

So they had just one more day of happiness together, and that night they dreamed the sweetest of dreams. When the man awoke in the morning he found himself lying on a rock. There was no sign of the house, and he was quite alone.

The Crane Wife
Japan

Once there was a man named Karoku. He lived with his seventy-year-old mother far back in the mountains, where he made charcoal for a living. One winter, as he was going to the village to buy some futon bedding, he saw a crane struggling in a trap where it had been caught.

Just as Karoku was stooping to release the poor crane, the man who had set the trap came running up. "What are you doing, interfering with other people's business?" he cried.

"I felt so sorry for the crane I thought I would let it go. Will you sell it to me? Here, I have the money I was going to use to buy a futon. Please take the money, and let me have the crane." The man agreed, and Karoku took the crane and immediately let if fly away free.

"Well," thought Karoku, returning home, "we may get cold tonight, but it can't be helped." When he got home, his mother asked what he had done with the futon. He replied, "I saw a crane caught in a trap. I felt so sorry for it that I used all the money to buy it and set it free."

"Well," his mother said, "since you have done it, I suppose that it is all right."

The next evening, just as night was falling, a beautiful young lady such as they had never seen before came to Karoku's house. "Please let me spend the night here," she asked, but Karoku refused, saying, "My little hut is too poor." She replied, "No, I do not mind; please, I implore you, let me stay," until finally he consented, and she was allowed to spend the night.

During the evening she said, "I have something I should like to discuss with you," and when Karoku asked what it was, she replied, "I beg of you, please make me your wife."

Karoku, greatly surprised, said, "This is the first time in my life that I have seen such a beautiful woman as you. I am a very poor man; I do not even know where my next meal is coming from; how could I ever take you as my wife?"

"Please do not refuse," she pleaded, "please take me as your wife."

"Well, you beg me so much, I don't know what to do," he replied. When his mother heard this, she said to her, "Since you insist, you may become my son's bride. Please stay here and work hard." Soon preparations were made, and they were married.

Sometime after this his wife said, "Please put me in a cabinet and leave me there for three days. Close the door tightly and be sure not to open it and look at me." Her husband put her in a cabinet, and on the fourth day, she came out. "It must have been very unpleasant in there," he said. "I was worried about you. Hurry and have something to eat."

"All right," she said. After she finished eating she said, "Karoku, Karoku, please take the cloth that I wove while in the cabinet and sell it for two thousand *ryo*." Saying this, she took a bolt of cloth from the cabinet and gave it to her husband.

He took it to the lord of the province, who, when he saw

it, said, "This is very beautiful material, I will pay you two or even three thousand *ryo* for it. Can you bring me another bolt like it?"

"I must ask my wife if she can weave another," Karoku replied.

"Oh, you need not ask her; it is all right if only you agree. I will give you the money for it now," the lord said.

Karoku returned home and told his wife what the lord had said. "Just give me time and I'll weave another bolt," she said. "This time please shut me in the cabinet for one week. During that time you must be sure not to open the door and look at me." And so he shut her in the cabinet again.

By the time the week was nearly over, Karoku became very worried about his wife. On the last day of the week, he opened the door to see if she was all right. There inside the cabinet was a crane, naked after having pulled out all her beautiful long feathers. She was using her feathers to weave the cloth and was just at the point of finishing it.

The crane cried out, "I have finished the cloth, but since you have seen who I really am, I am afraid that you can no longer love me. I must return to my home. I am not a person, but the crane whom you rescued. Please take the cloth to the lord as you promised."

After she had said this, the crane silently turned toward the west. When she did this, thousands of cranes appeared, and taking her with them, they all flew out of sight.

Karoku had become a rich man, but he wanted to see his beloved wife so badly that he could not bear it. He searched for her throughout Japan until he was exhausted. One day as he was sitting on the seashore resting, he saw an old man alone in a rowboat, approaching from the open ocean. "How strange," thought Karoku. "Where could he be coming from; there are no islands near here." As he sat in bewilderment, the boat landed on the beach. Karoku called out, "Grandfather, where did you come from?"

"I came from an island called 'The Robe of Crane Feathers,'" the old man replied.

"Would you please take me to that island?" asked Karoku.

The old man quickly agreed, and Karoku climbed into the boat. The boat sped over the water, and in no time they had arrived at a beautiful white beach. They landed, and when Karoku got out of the boat and turned around, the boat and the old man had vanished from sight.

Karoku walked up the beach and soon came to a beautiful pond. In the middle of the pond was an island, and there on the island was the naked crane. She was surrounded by a myriad of cranes, for she was queen of the cranes.

Karoku stayed a short while and was given a feast. Afterward the old man with the boat returned, and Karoku was taken back to his home.

The Lizard Husband
Indonesia

Once there was an old woman who lived alone in the jungle and had a lizard which she brought up as her child. When he was full grown, he said to her, "Grandmother, go to the house of Lise, where there are seven sisters, and ask for the eldest of these for me as a wife." The old woman did as the lizard requested, and taking the bridal gifts with her, went off. But when she came near the house, Lise saw her and said, "Look, here comes Lizard's grandmother with a bridal present. Who would want to marry a lizard! Not I."

The old woman arrived at the foot of the ladder, as-
cended it, and sat down in Lise's house, whereupon the eldest sister gave her betel, and when her mouth was red
from chewing it, asked, "What have you come for, Grandmother? Why do you come to us?"

"Well, Granddaughter, I have come for this: to present a
bridal gift; perhaps it will be accepted, perhaps not. That is
what I have come to see."

As soon as she had spoken, the eldest indicated her refusal by getting up and giving the old woman a blow that
knocked her across to the door, following this with another
that rolled her down the ladder. The old woman picked
herself up and went home.

When she had reached her house, the lizard inquired,
"How did your visit succeed?" She replied, "O! Alas! I was
afraid and almost killed. The gift was not accepted; the eldest would not accept it; it seems she has no use for you because you are only a lizard."

"Do not be disturbed," said he, "go tomorrow and ask
for the second sister." The old woman did not refuse, but
went the following morning, only to be denied as before.
Each day she went again to another of the sisters until the
turn of the youngest came. This time the girl did not listen
to what Lise said and did not strike the old woman or drive
her away, but agreed to become Lizard's wife. The old
woman was delighted and said that after seven nights she
and her son would come.

When this time had passed, the grandmother arrived,
carrying the lizard in a basket. Kapapitoe, the youngest sister, laid down a mat for the old woman to sit on while she
spread out the wedding gifts, whereupon the young bride
gave her food; and after she had eaten and gone home, the
lizard remained as Kapapitoe's husband.

The other sisters took pains to show their disgust. When
they returned home at night, they would wipe the mud off

their feet on Lizard's back and would say, "Pitoe can't prepare any garden, she must stay and take care of her lizard." But Kapapitoe would say, "Keep quiet. I shall take him down to the river and wash off the mud."

After a while the older sisters got ready to make a clearing for a garden, and one day, when they had gone to work, the lizard said to his wife, "We have too much to bear. Your sisters tease us too much. Come, let us go and make a garden. Carry me in a basket on your back, wife, and gather also seven empty coconut shells." His wife agreed, put her husband in a basket, and after collecting the seven shells, went to the place which they were to make ready for their garden. Then the lizard said, "Put me down on the ground, wife, so that I can run about," and thus he scurried around, lashing the grass and trees with his tail and covering a whole mountainside in the course of the day. With one blow he felled a tree, cut it up by means of the sharp points on his skin, set the pieces afire, and burned the whole area, making the clearing smooth and good.

Then he said to Kapapitoe, "Make a little seat for me, so that I can go and sit on it," and when this was done, he ordered the seven coconut shells to build a house for him, after which he was carried home by his wife.

The older sisters returning that evening saw the new clearing and wondered at it, perceiving that it was ready for planting. When they got home they said to their sister, "You can't go thus to the planting feast of Ta Datoe. Your husband is only a lizard," and again they wiped their feet on him.

The next day Lizard and his wife went once more to their clearing and saw that the house had already been built for them by the coconut shells, which had turned into slaves. The lizard said, "Good, tomorrow evening we will hold the preliminary planting festival, and the next day a planting feast." Ordering his seven slaves to prepare much food for the occasion, he said to his wife, "Let us go to the river and get ready."

But on arriving at the stream, they bathed far apart, and the lizard, taking off his animal disguise, became a very handsome man dressed in magnificent garments.

When he came for his wife, she at first did not recognize him, but at last she was convinced, and after she had been given costly new clothes and ornaments, they returned to Lise's house.

As they came back, the preliminary planting festival had begun, and many people were gathered, including Kapapi-toe's elder sisters, Lise, and the old woman. The six sisters said, "Tell us, Grandmother, who is that coming? She looks so handsome, and her sarong rustles as if rain were falling. The hem of her sarong goes up and down every moment as it touches her ankles."

The old woman replied, "That is your youngest sister, and here comes her husband also." Then overcome with jealousy, the six sisters ran to meet their handsome brother-in-law and vied with each other for the privilege of carrying his betel sack, saying "I want to hold the *sirih*-sack of my brother-in-law."

He, however, went and sat down, and the six went to sit beside him to take him away from their youngest sister. But the lizard would have none of them.

Next day was the planting, and his sisters-in-law would not let the lizard go in company with his wife, but took possession of him; this made him angry. Accordingly, when Lise and the sisters were asleep, the lizard got up, waked Ka-papitoe, and taking a stone, laid four pieces of bark upon it and repeated a charm: "If there is power in the wish of the six sisters who wipe their feet on me, then I shall, when I open my eyes, be sitting on the ground just as I am now. But if my wish has power, when I open my eyes, I shall be sitting in my house and looking down on all other houses."

When he opened his eyes, he was seated in his house high up on the mountain, for the stone had grown into a great rock, and his house was on top of it. His sisters-in-law tried to climb the cliff, but in vain, and so had to give up, while he and his wife, Kapapitoe, lived happily ever after.

The Wolf Dream
China

In the province of Zhili there was an old man named Bai whose eldest son served as an official in the south. The son had been gone for three years, during which time old Bai received no word from him. As it happened, a relative named Ding came to visit the old man. Ding had psychic powers, and the old man liked to question him about the occult, though he never quite believed the strange things that Ding told him.

A few days later when Bai was asleep he saw Ding approach him and invite him to go for a stroll. They walked together outside the city gate and into a moat, where Ding pointed to a large gate and said, "This is where your nephew lives." The old man did indeed have a nephew, the son of his elder sister, but he was an official in Shanxi. The old man said, "How can this be?" Ding replied, "If you don't believe it, go inside and see for yourself."

So old Bai went inside, and there was his nephew sitting in a great hall, wearing the gauze cap and red robe of an official, and surrounded by armed guards. Ding pulled the old man aside and said to him, "Your son's tribunal is not far from here. Would you like to go see him?"

Bai assented, and in a moment they found themselves in front of another great hall. "Let's go in," said Ding. Old Bai looked in; but all he could see was a huge wolf blocking the entryway, and he was so frightened he dared not go in. "Let's go in," said Ding again. The old man did go through one set of doors, but when his eyes met a whole room full of wolves surrounding a veritable mountain of white bones, he was even more frightened; and only with the greatest reluctance would he follow at a safe distance behind Ding.

The old man's son just happened to be passing by at that moment, and he was overjoyed to see his father. He invited the two guests to sit with him for a moment, and he ordered his servants to prepare a meal for them. Suddenly a huge wolf entered carrying a dead man in his mouth. The old man trembled with terror as he heard his son say, "Take him to the kitchen and cook him up for us to eat." With pounding heart the old man tried to flee, but his way was blocked by a pack of wolves.

Suddenly the wolves began to howl and run about in confusion, some hiding beneath a bed and some cowering under a table. The old man thought this very strange, and could not understand what was happening. In a moment, two warriors in golden armor carrying a black rope entered the hall, and proceeded to tie up his son, who fell to the ground and turned into a tiger displaying a mouthful of sharp teeth. One of the warriors drew a precious sword and was about to kill the tiger, but the other said, "Do not be so hasty! This should take place in the fourth month of next year. For the moment why don't you just knock out his teeth?" So he took a metal cudgel and knocked out the tiger's teeth, scattering them here and there all over the hall. The tiger let out a long roar which shook the very rocks and hills.

The old man was frightened nearly out of his wits, when

he woke up and realized that it had all been a dream. He asked one of his servants to summon Ding, but Ding refused to come. Then he wrote down the dream, and wrote a letter of warning to his son, and asked his younger son to deliver it for him.

When the younger son arrived at his brother's place he was surprised to see that the latter was missing his front teeth; and when he asked the reason, his brother replied that he lost them when he fell off a horse, after he had been drinking. The date of this accident was the same as the date of his father's dream. The younger brother then brought out his father's letter. The elder brother blanched as he read it, but he said, "This is just a random dream, and the events are purely coincidental. There is no cause for alarm." And since he was involved in an important case at the moment, he put the dream out of his mind.

The younger brother stayed there several days and saw that his brother's associates were a group of evil fellows who gave and took bribes and engaged in every kind of degenerate behavior day and night. He implored his brother to put a stop to such actions, but his brother said, "You live in the countryside and don't understand how things are done in official circles. In order to be promoted one has to attend to the interests of one's superiors, not to the common people. If one tries to be a good official and look after the needs of the people, how can one expect to impress one's superiors?"

The younger brother knew there was nothing he could do, so he returned home and reported everything to his father. The old man wept. Then he gathered up all his wealth and distributed it to the poor, and prayed to the gods that when they rained down destruction on his wayward son they would spare the rest of his family.

The next year news came that his elder son had received a promotion and was moving to another post. Crowds of well-wishers came to congratulate the old man, but he took to his bed and pretended to be sick in order not to receive them.

Shortly thereafter he received news that his son had been waylaid by robbers on his journey home, and that all the men in his party had been killed. The old man crawled out of his bed and said, "The anger of the ghosts has been poured out on him alone, and the rest of the family has been spared." Then he lit candles and incense, and offered thanks to the gods.

When friends and relatives came to comfort the old man they thought that the news might not be reliable, but the old man had no doubts at all, and proceeded to set a date for his son's burial. But in fact his son had not died. Back in the fourth month he had gone to take up his new position, and just as he had left the city he had met a band of robbers and had given them all his money. The robbers said, "We have come to avenge the common people of this district; surely you don't think this is sufficient!" Then they cut off his head.

One of the robbers asked, "Which of you is Si Dacheng?" Now Si Dacheng was the leader of the corrupt officials, and was constantly goading his master to carry out evil deeds. The people in the entourage pointed out Si Dacheng, and the robbers immediately put him to death. There were four other corrupt retainers who helped the officials exploit the common people, and the robbers killed them too, then left—not without taking all the money and valuables from their victims' pockets.

An official walking past asked, "Who was killed here just now?" Some of the servants in the entourage answered, "It was an official named Bai." The official said, "This must be the son of old man Bai. The old man should not suffer the pain of his son's cruel death. Perhaps we can put his head back on." Then he put the head back on the corpse's neck, saying, "This is a crooked man, and we should not put his head on straight, but let his chin hang over his shoulder." Then he left.

After a while the son regained consciousness. Fortunately his wife had come to recover his body, and when she saw that he was still breathing she poured a little water into his mouth, and he drank it. But he and his wife stayed in an inn, and dared not go home in their impoverished state.

After half a year the father heard what had happened and sent his younger son to go fetch the elder brother. But although he had regained his life, his head was so twisted that he could see his spine, and people treated him as someone not quite human.

As for the old man's nephew, he was an official with an excellent reputation, and within a year he was promoted to the Imperial Censorate. Everything in the old man's dream had turned out to be true.

Escaping from the Ogre
Indonesia

Two women once went fishing, and coming to a river, one said to the other, "There are many fish in that pool; reach down for them." But when the other stooped for the fish, the first woman gave her a push, so that she fell into the water, and then she held her under with a forked stick. Great bubbles came up as the victim struggled, but at last they ceased and she was drowned, whereupon the murderess drew out the body, cut off some flesh, put it in a bamboo vessel, and going home, set the vessel on the fire to cook.

Now the dead woman had two children, a boy and a girl, and they asked the wicked woman what she was cooking. She replied, "Fish and eels," and then saying that she was going back to her comrade, she told the children to watch what she had left to cook. After she had left, the flesh of the children's mother soon began to boil, saying, "I am your mother here!" The girl, who heard this, called to her brother, and he came and listened, whereupon the children said to one another, "We must run away, whether we meet with good fortune or bad."

The wicked woman now came home, and the children asked her where their mother was, to which she replied that her companion was still busy smoking the fish which they had caught, and that she was now going to take her some food.

Then she went off again, telling the children to look after her own little one, who was younger than they. But when she had gone, the two children took the young child of the wicked woman, put it in the pan to cook over the fire, and ran away.

They went across seven mountains and seven valleys and came to a river which was full of crocodiles, so they could not pass. A bird saw them, however, and learning of their trouble, told them of a log that lay athwart the river some distance upstream; and after they were safe on the other side, the bird flew across the log, which it nearly severed with its beak.

The wicked woman returning to the house and finding her child all shriveled and burned, set out at once in pursuit, saying, "You who did this shall die this very day." By and by she came to the log by which the children had crossed, but when she attempted to follow them, it broke under her weight. She fell into the stream, and the crocodiles ate her up.

The bird now told the children that they must not follow

the path that led to the left, but must take that going to the right. They did not heed this advice, however, and turning off to the left, after a time they met Kine-kine-boro, an ogre who had a carrying basket on his back in which a man was stuck head down.

The children called out to the ogre, "Good grandfather, grandfather, look here!" and he, saying "Ha! From the beginning of the world, I have never had any children or grandchildren," looked around and called to them, "Grandchildren, come here!"

Accordingly they went with him to his house, and after they had been there half a moon, they said to him, "Grandfather, haven't you an axe?" "Yes," said he, "Here is the axe, what do you want with it?" "We want to make a canoe to play with."

So they went to cut down a tree, and Kine-kine-boro felled one and carried it home for them. But next day, when the ogre and his wife had gone off to seek men to eat, the children finished their canoe, loaded it with rice and precious goods belonging to the ogre, and paddled away.

Not long after, Kine-kine-boro and his wife returned, and as they had not found any men, they went to the enclosure where the children were kept, intending to eat them. Since, however, their intended victims were not there, the ogre and his wife climbed into a tree to look for them, but could not see them.

By climbing a very tall tree Kine-kine-boro at last spied them, the sail of their canoe being a mere speck on the horizon. Then he took his hair and from it plaited a rope, which he threw after the canoe like a lasso, so that finally he caught the little boat and began to pull it in.

The two children tried to cut the rope, but in vain. Until, after sawing at it for a long time with a curved knife, it broke; whereupon—so tightly had the rope been stretched—the tree, in whose top Kine-kine-boro was, snapped back. Seven times it swayed toward the land, and seven times toward the sea; and Kine-kine-boro fell from the tree upon his wife who was below. They both burst with a noise like thunder and died, but the children got safely away.

The Pedlar's Son
China

In Hubei there was an old man who worked as an itinerant pedlar. Once while he was away from home, his wife dreamed that a man came into her bed and slept with her. When she woke up she found that there was in fact a young man lying next to her. He did not look quite like an ordinary man, and she realized that he was a fox spirit. In an instant he jumped out of bed and disappeared through the wall, without even opening the door.

That evening she asked one of her women servants to stay with her in her room. She had a ten-year-old son who usually slept in another bed, but now she asked him to sleep in the same bed with her too. Late that night, when the servant and the boy were asleep, the fox spirit returned. The woman muttered something in her dream, waking the servant, who called out in alarm, frightening away the fox spirit.

The next day she seemed distracted, as if in a trance. In the evening she did not dare blow out the candle, and she warned her son not to sleep too deeply. But the servant and the boy nodded off to sleep, and when they woke up the woman was not there. At first they thought she had merely gone out to relieve herself, but after a while, when she had not returned, they began to worry. The servant was afraid to go looking for her, but the boy took the lamp and searched all around, and finally found his mother sleeping naked in another room. He helped her up, and she seemed not to be ashamed of her condition.

She became a madwoman, sometimes singing, sometimes crying, sometimes cursing loudly. She would not consent to have anyone sleep in the same room with her, not even the servant or the boy. When she cried out in her sleep, her son would light the lamp and look in on her, but she would become angry and curse him.

But the boy was very clever, and he learned masonry, and built a wall of bricks and stones which covered the windows. People tried to stop him, but he would not pay attention to them. Once someone took down one of the stones, but he just rolled on the ground shouting and crying and raising such a fuss that no one dared stop him again. After he blocked off the windows he started filling in cracks in the walls; and when he finished that he got the chopping knife from the kitchen and sharpened it to a fine edge. No one knew what he was up to, and most people ascribed his behavior to a childish naughtiness.

That evening the boy hid the knife under his jacket, covered the lamp, and waited. When his mother began to talk in her sleep, he quickly uncovered the lamp, stood in the doorway, and called out to her. Hearing no response, he left the doorway and pretended to go outside to relieve himself. Suddenly he saw something like a fox streaking out through the door. Quickly he chopped at it with the knife, but was only able to cut off two or three inches of its tail. It ran off, leaving a trail of blood behind it.

His mother cursed him, but he pretended not to hear, and he hoped that the fox had suffered enough of a scare not to come again. In the morning he followed the trail of blood over the wall and into the neighbor's garden. When the fox failed to return that evening, the boy was very happy, but his mother lay there stiffly as though she were dead.

After some time the pedlar returned. When he went to see his wife she cursed him and treated him like a stranger. The boy told his father what had happened while he was gone, so the pedlar went to an herbal doctor to get some medicine to cure his wife's condition. When he gave her the medicine to drink, she dashed it to the ground, cursing. But the pedlar secretly put some medicine in her soup, and she ate it. In a few days she had gradually returned to her former self.

One evening the pedlar woke up to find that his wife was not at his side. He and his son found her in another room, and from then on her former madness returned and she refused to sleep in the same room with her husband. He locked the doors of all the other rooms in the house, but somehow when she approached them the doors opened by themselves. The pedlar had done all he could, and his only recourse was to ask a Daoist priest to cast out the evil in the house; but even the priest's prayers had no effect.

One day, when the sun was about to set, the boy secretly slipped into his neighbor's garden and hid among the weeds, hoping to find out what had happened to the fox. As the moon was beginning to rise, he suddenly heard voices. Quietly he parted the tall grasses where he was hiding, and looking out, he saw two young men there drinking wine. Then a servant with a long beard, dressed in dark brown, came over carrying a pot of wine. The two were talking very quietly, and it was hard to make out what they were saying. After a while the boy heard one of the men say, "Tomorrow you can bring a jug of rice wine."

After a while the two men left, leaving only the bearded servant in the garden. The servant took off his clothing and went to sleep on a stone slab in the middle of the garden.

Looking carefully, the pedlar's son could see that his limbs looked like those of a man, but a tail extended from his lower back. The boy wanted to return home, but fearing that he would waken the fox he spent all night in the garden. Early the next morning when he heard the two men talking quietly in the bamboo grove he made his way back home. When his father asked where he had been he replied that he had been at the neighbor's house.

As it happened, when the boy went with his father to the market that day he saw a fox tail in the hatter's shop, and he asked his father to buy it for him. At first his father refused, but as the boy pulled at his sleeve and whined and carried on, the father finally could stand it no longer and bought it for him. While his father was selling his wares in the market the boy played by his side, but when the father was not looking the boy stole some money and went to the wineshop to buy a bottle of rice wine, which he had the wineshop hold there for him.

The boy had an uncle who was a hunter, whose home was nearby, and he went to see him. The uncle was out, but the aunt said to him, "How is your mother's condition?" He replied, "She is much better these days, but there is a rat which has been gnawing on our clothes, which makes her very angry, and she has sent me here to get some animal poison from you." His aunt got about a pennyweight of poison from a cabinet and wrapped it up and gave it to him. He thought it might not be enough, and while she went into another room to prepare a bowl of noodles for him to eat, he opened the cabinet and took out another handful of the poison, wrapped it in a piece of paper, and hid it inside his jacket.

Then he called to his aunt, "My father is waiting for me at the market, so please don't trouble yourself to make me any noodles," and he ran off. He secretly put the poison in the bottle of rice wine, then played for a while in the marketplace, and returned home. When his father asked where he had been, he said, "At my uncle's."

The boy continued to follow his father to the market and play by his side. One day he saw the bearded servant in the crowd. He made his way over to where he was and struck up a conversation with him, asking, "Where do you live?" "In North Village." The man asked the boy the same question, to which he replied, "In a cave."

The bearded man was surprised and asked how he could live in a cave. "Our family has lived there for generations," he said, "hasn't yours?" The bearded man was taken aback, and asked him his surname. "My family name is Fox," he replied. "Haven't we met somewhere before? You were with those two young men, or have you forgotten?" The bearded man looked at him carefully and could not tell whether to trust him or not.

But the boy loosened his trousers a bit, revealing the tail which he had hidden inside. "We have mixed our blood with humans and only this blasted thing remains," he said. "What are you doing in the market?" the bearded man asked. The boy replied, "My father sent me here to buy some wine." The man said he was also there to buy wine. "Have you bought it yet?" the boy asked. "We are very poor, so usually we steal it," said the man. "That is a thankless task, and not without danger." "I know," said the man, "but my masters have ordered me to do it, and I have to obey." "Who are your masters?" the boy asked.

"Those two young men you saw me with. They are brothers—one is connected with one of the women in the Wang family outside the north gate, and the other lives in a pedlar's house in East Village.

"The pedlar has a bothersome son who cut off his tail, and it took ten days to heal, but now it is better and he has gone back there. But I have to be going now and find some wine."

"It is hard work stealing wine, and better to buy it. I have just bought some wine myself, which I am keeping in the wineshop, and I would be glad to give it to you. I still have some money left, so don't worry about me." The man said, "I am sorry, but I have nothing to give you in return." The boy replied, "We are two of a kind, and we need not keep a tally of debts and favors. I will come visit you when I have some free time, and have a drink with you." Then they went together to get the wine, and each returned to his own home.

That evening his mother slept peacefully, and the boy knew that something had happened. He told his father what he had done, and the two of them went to the neighbor's garden to investigate. There they saw two foxes lying dead in a pavilion, and one fox lying dead in the grass, blood flowing from its mouth. The wine bottle was still lying there, and when they shook it they found that it still contained some wine. The father was amazed and said, "Why didn't you tell me about this earlier?" His son replied, "If word had leaked out and they had found out about it, my plan would not have worked." The father said with pride, "My son is truly a master fox-slayer." Then father and son took the three fox corpses away, and they could see the scar on the tail of one of them.

From this time on their household was peaceful. But the woman was frightfully thin, and as she gradually realized what had happened to her she developed a coughing illness, and not long afterward she died. The woman from the Wang family who had also been haunted by a fox recovered. The pedlar knew that his son was not an ordinary child, and taught him horsemanship and archery, and he became a skillful soldier.

The Story of Nai Prasop
Thailand

Long ago in Supanburi, about the middle of the fifteenth century, there lived the son of a wealthy old lady, who, to please his mother, had agreed to enter the priesthood. His name was Nai Prasop. When the appointed day arrived, his mother and their friends and relatives took him in their midst, clothed all in white, and went in procession to hand him over to the head priest of the temple he was about to enter, and to make a little merit on their own behalf.

Among those who joined the procession and followed in his mother's train was one of her female slaves, who, having a girl infant still suckling, took the child with her on her hip. When the procession arrived at the temple, as she did not wish to carry the child about, the slave placed a cradle under the cell that Nai Prasop was about to occupy and put the infant in it to sleep.

Now it happened that at the same time as Nai Prasop was initiated into the priesthood a certain astrologer of great repute among the townsfolk came to the temple to atone for his sins. When the ceremony of initiation was over and his folk had left him alone, Nai Prasop invited the astrologer into his cell. He asked him to consult his horoscope and reveal what his fate would be, especially the name of his future wife.

The astrologer complied, and, having made his calculations, told Nai Prasop three things: first, that his future bride would be the child of a slave; secondly, that she was still an infant; and thirdly, that at that very moment she was on a lower physical plane than he. Having uttered these predictions, the astrologer took his leave.

Left to himself, Nai Prasop was very downcast and sore

at heart at the thought that his wife was to be the child of a slave and not one of his own standing and position, but he accepted the omen without hesitation, for he had great faith in the astrologer's powers. As he lay brooding on these troubling thoughts he suddenly looked through a hole in the floor of his cell and observed the slave's infant lying on its back in a cradle fast asleep.

Seeing the child of his mother's slave lying directly beneath him, it came upon him with a sudden shock that here was the future bride predicted for him by the astrologer.

Then an evil thought came into his head, and he said to himself, "There can be no doubt about it: this is the infant to whom the astrologer referred. If I let her grow up to a marriageable age, his prediction will come true and I shall have to take her to wife. But I cannot and will not do it. I should be covered with shame, and could never look my own or my mother's friends in the face again. But now's my chance—the mother's away, and there's no one about. I must get rid of the child somehow while I can."

He was not really an evil-hearted boy, but his belief in the astrologer was strong, and opportunity is the lover of temptation. So, searching about, he found a house knife used for cutting bamboo strips, and, inserting the blade in the hole in the floor just over the child's stomach, let the knife fall with a violent jerk of his hand. He thought the point would pierce the region of the infant's heart, but Fate decreed that the child's hour was not yet come.

It happened that the knife swerved in falling and the shaft struck the side of the hole in the floor. So it missed the spot it was meant to strike, and the point of the knife entered the groin below the child's stomach instead. The wound it caused, although not fatal, was still a serious one, and the child sent up such a scream of pain that its mother heard the noise at once and came rushing to see what had happened.

When she found the knife sticking in her child's groin and the child itself lying in a pool of blood, she was overcome with grief and anguish. She gave no heed then to who had done the deed, but plucked the knife from the wound and carried the child off as fast as she could go. Seeking out her mistress, she told her the story and showed her the child, and between them they washed and dressed the wound. Fortunately the infant was a healthy one, and the wound soon began to heal, and after some little time nothing was left but a scar to mark the spot.

Naturally the affair caused some little stir among the household, and it was not long before the slave found out the truth: that the son of her mistress was the author of the crime, and that he had tried to kill her child because an astrologer had predicted that she was to be his future bride. But even so, what could she do? She was only a slave, and she had no actual proof of his guilt.

She could not go to her mistress with a tale of suspicion, and she therefore made up her mind that the only thing to do, as she could not bear to live near the son anymore, was to try and discover some means of leaving the household. Luckily for her, she was able to find a friend to redeem her own and her husband's debts, and so she left the family, taking her husband and child with her. From that time they disappeared as completely as if the earth had swallowed them up. Neither Nai Prasop nor his mother could find any trace of their whereabouts, in spite of all their diligent inquiry.

Now it happened that, some years after this, all the merit that the mother of Nai Prasop had acquired in the past spent its strength, and she fell on evil times. All her servants ran away and left her; her cattle, horses, and buffaloes died, her boats and rafts were lost, her wealth was gone, and there was nothing left for her in her old age but to lie down and die. The loss of his mother and wealth was a heavy blow to Nai Prasop.

He had now no natural guardian, no one to look after his daily wants and supply him with his food, or candles, or betel. Although he was still in the priesthood, he began to feel his position acutely as he saw that the people around him no longer regarded him with the same favor as before. By becoming a priest he had brought merit to himself and his family, but now it was evident that he had no more merit within him, and he determined to retire from the priesthood and go into secular life.

But when he came out into the world again there was nothing that he could do. He had never learnt a trade, and had no money with which to establish himself in any business. So he wandered about from place to place, looking for any kind of work which folk might give him out of kindness, to keep his body and soul alive. In the course of years he visited many towns and many villages, but never found a home in which to settle; until he happened one day, in a certain city, to enter the house of a rich merchant, to whom he offered himself as a servant. By chance the merchant had recently lost a servant and was seeking to replace him; and, as soon as he saw Nai Prasop, he liked the look of him.

It will be remembered that Nai Prasop was the son of wealthy parents, and although he had fallen low in the world, he had not forgotten his former estate, and still retained the breeding his mother had taught him. His manners were good, and, finding the merchant willing to take him in, he resolved to do his utmost to serve and please him. So he entered the house as a servant, and, by his diligence and honesty and bearing, soon became a favorite of the family, so much so that after a certain time the daughter of the merchant fell in love with him, and he with her. When the parents of the girl discovered this, such was their regard for Nai Prasop that they raised no objection to the marriage, and at the proper season Nai Prasop and their daughter became man and wife amid great rejoicings.

They continued to live with her parents as before and were as happy as the day is long, until one night, when they had been married some little while, Nai Prasop noticed that his wife had a scar on her groin, as if she had been stabbed with a knife. At once his mind went back to the day of his terrible crime, for which he had suffered much remorse ever since; but, hiding his suspicions, he became sympathetic and loving towards his wife and tenderly asked her to tell him how it had happened and what was the cause.

His wife had, of course, heard the tale many times from her mother's lips, and this is the story she related to her husband: "Many years ago, dear, when I was very small, my father and mother were the slaves of an old lady who lived in Supanburi. On a certain day when the son of the old lady was to be initiated into the priesthood, my mother went with the procession to the temple, and, as I was still an infant, she took me with her as well, and put me into a cradle beneath the cell which the son would occupy as a priest. While I was asleep there, an astrologer came to visit the son in his cell and foretold that I was to be his future wife.

"In his disgust at such a thought, the son took a knife and tried to kill me, but by a happy accident the knife struck me in the groin and did not give me a mortal wound, and so I escaped and lived to become your wife, dear husband. But my father and mother refused to live any longer in the old lady's family, and, having found a friend to redeem them, left her and came to settle in this city. My father set up as a merchant, and by his honesty and ability has risen to the position in which you see him now."

Nai Prasop listened intently to his wife's tale, and almost at the first word recognized that she was the infant whom he had tried to kill. He thought to himself, "By the Lord Buddha, to think that I was the son of a good family, that once my parents were people of wealth, which I imagined would last forever. I never thought of this business of merit and demerit, which is able to change our lives in the twinkling of an eye, and which actually brought me down to a pretty low estate. And so I thought to escape my fate by killing the infant, who is now my wife. In those days she was on a lower plane than I, but on what a far lower plane am I now than she, and all through the merit and demerit we have earned! What a fool I was and a scoundrel!"

But he did not tell his thoughts to his wife.

The Dream at Nam Kha
Vietnam

For the third time in a row the ambitious student Lu Sinh had failed in the triennial competitive examinations. Bad fortune seemed to pursue him ceaselessly, so that he had to suffer the bitterness of observing other students, less well endowed mentally than he and much less scholarly in their habits, pass the examinations and move on to success and fortune.

With great sadness in his heart, Lu Sinh left the capital to return to his native village. He traveled on foot, a light pack dangling from the end of a stick over his shoulder.

While crossing the region of Nam Kha he was surprised by a sudden downpour of rain in the mountains. He climbed into a grotto to take refuge, and there discovered an old Daoist.

The hermit had his unexpected guest sit down on the only piece of furniture in the cave, a bed of smooth stone. While watching over the cooking of a potful of millet, he informed Lu Sinh courteously about the condition of the road that lay ahead of him on his journey. Lu Sinh, in his turn, began to confide to the aged recluse the sad tale of his disappointments; he also told of his intention of starting all over again to study, of his hopes and ambitions for the future. To all this the hermit listened in silence. Then he invited Lu Sinh to stretch out on the stone bed beside the fire and take a much-needed rest before continuing his journey.

Three years later, Lu Sinh met success in his struggle. He received the degree of First Scholar of the Empire. From the beginning of that day to its end, everything was gloriously and memorably arranged.

First of all, there were unforgettable formal ceremonies, marked by the proclamation of Lu Sinh's name by a herald flourishing a trumpet of shining copper before a huge crowd assembled for the occasion. Then Lu Sinh, in the solemn court dress of a great mandarin, and seated nobly astride a white horse, led a procession across the capital city and on as far as his own village, where for several days festivals and merrymaking went on without interruption.

Subsequently there followed for Lu Sinh the exercise of high public office; marriage to a princess, the prettiest of the emperor's daughters; then, in a few years, the births of handsome children; and eventual elevation to the rank of First Minister. It was indeed a rapid rise to the pinnacle of riches and honors, and there Lu Sinh maintained himself for fifteen years.

Then there came a sudden invasion of the country by the barbarians. The first battles were disastrous for the empire. But then Lu Sinh was called to the supreme command, and he succeeded in repulsing the enemy. Next, he led his troops in turn in an invasion of the enemy's territory, and killed the king. However, the wild charm of the queen of that land so enthralled him that he decided to remain with her. Carried away completely by this new and irresistible passion, Lu Sinh completely forgot his wife, his own fireside, even his duty to his king and country.

In vain did the emperor summon him home. When Lu Sinh ignored the imperial command, an expedition was sent against him. Lu Sinh became an insurgent, determined to resist his ruler's troops by force; but his own lieutenants betrayed him and handed him over to justice. Despite the tears and pleadings of Lu Sinh's wife, the emperor condemned him to death.

On the night preceding his execution, Lu Sinh passed the hours recalling his entire life: his poverty-stricken childhood, his work as a student, his brilliant rise to the very pinnacle of success and power, his happiness, then the intoxicating passion that had destroyed him, his misconduct, his sudden fall. . . .

Lu Sinh opened his eyes. He was in the mountain grotto, lying on the stone bed. Near him, crouching on the ground, the old recluse slowly stirred his millet porridge. Only the light sound of his spoon on the bottom of the kettle, scarcely more perceptible than the singing of the fire, disturbed the silence of the mountain. The rain had ceased.

"Young man," said the hermit, "you have had a long dream, but my porridge is not yet cooked. Just one more minute—then give me the pleasure of sharing my modest meal."

何仙姑

Cleverness and
Foolishness

People all over the world admire the clever and laugh at the foolish, and delight in telling stories of both. Stories of clever people seem at first glance to be similar in both form and function to animal trickster tales, but they differ from trickster tales in that they have to do with social situations rather than physical encounters. The clever person in these stories typically wins a dispute over property or money, but does not try to kill his opponent.

Innate foolishness can take many forms, including literal-mindedness, forgetfulness, and applying social rules inappropriately. Stories about simple fools approach pure comedy. But some other stories in this group have a didactic tone. Greed figures into several of them, causing characters of ordinary mental capacity to forsake their common sense when tempted by wealth, thereby making them easy targets for clever characters who understand this human weakness only too well.

East Asian cultures have a special category of stories

about wise judges or magistrates, who, like Solomon, solve difficult cases through unconventional and clever means. "The River God's Wife," "Ooka the Wise," and the stories of "Wise Magistrates" which follow all belong to this popular type. The stories are particularly effective when the judge uses the plaintiff's own logic to reach a judgment against him.

The Glass Stopper
Thailand

Not long ago there lived in Bangkok a man of standing and rank named Phra Chamnan, who was well known as a dealer in gems. He was eagerly sought after by the princes and nobles, and even more by their wives, for the selection and purchase of jewels, and his reputation as an appraiser of precious stones was such that you could not find his equal anywhere, search where you would.

There was also a fellow of no education or substance named Nai Kroh Dee, who, though of the lower orders, was yet on intimate terms with the dealer in gems, and visited him frequently. Now Kroh Dee had found by chance a small glass stopper which was broken at the base. Even so, it was a piece of well-cut crystal about the size of a berry, with a good water, and when the base had been ground down so as to remove all traces of the damage, and all the corners made sharp so that it had no similarity to a stopper, it certainly had, to the eye of a casual observer, the appearance of a large well-cut diamond.

This stopper, well wrapped in cloth, Kroh Dee took to Phra Chamnan one day and said, "I have brought with me

to show you a very ancient diamond, which has been carefully treasured in my family for generations. Now my
mother has died and left me this gem as my share of the in-
heritance. But frankly I do not know what to do with it. It
is far too big and too fine in quality for me to wear. Yet it's
no use my keeping it stored away, and besides I am a poor
man, and must needs have money to maintain myself. And
so I have brought this valuable stone to you, and would ask
you to be kind enough to sell it for me if you can. I do not
ask you to buy it yourself, but you are a well-known dealer,
so just let me deposit it with you, and if you get an opportunity, please do your best to sell it for me."

So saying, he very carefully undid the wrappings of cloth
and handed the 'gem' to Phra Chamnan to see. When he saw
it, Phra Chamnan laughed aloud, and, looking hard at Kroh
Dee, replied, "What do you mean, you rascal, by bringing
me a bottle stopper and calling it a beautiful gem!"

This accusation upset Kroh Dee, who denied that it was
a stopper, and affirmed stoutly that it was a very ancient
jewel.

"It has been in the possession of my grandmother and
great-grandmother, and has always been looked upon as a
most valuable heirloom; but anyhow, even if you don't believe me, please take it and sell it if you can. I don't ask you
to buy it, so you can think of it what you like."

Kroh Dee seemed so serious, and so affected by the
doubts raised as to the genuineness of his stone, that Phra
Chamnan agreed to receive it on deposit, and asked him
how much he wished to sell it for. But when Kroh Dee
replied that he wanted ten *chang*, Phra Chamnan could not
help bursting into laughter again and said shortly, "If you
were to value it at a *fuang*, perhaps somebody might buy it
to tie round the cat's neck. Still, never mind, it's of no particular importance anyway. I won't guarantee to sell it for
you, but you can leave it with me, and if anyone happens to
fancy it, I will see what I can do for you."

Thereupon Kroh Dee left the 'jewel' with Phra Chamnan, and went out of the shop.

Three months went by, and Phra Chamnan had almost forgotten the existence of the 'jewel,' when one day a Lao from the north came to visit him. The Lao told Phra Chamnan that he had been specially commissioned by the prince of his state to purchase a diamond of the first quality to be set as a pendant to a necklace which the prince wished to give to his principal wife. He had heard that Phra Chamnan was the most important gem dealer in Bangkok, and so he had naturally come to him first. Would he be good enough to show him what he had in the way of diamonds?

Phra Chamnan brought out all his finest diamonds for the Lao to examine, none of which was as large as the stopper belonging to Kroh Dee. The Lao looked at them all very carefully, admired some and criticized others. If the water was good, the gem was too small; or if the gem was the right size, then the water was poor. He could find none to satisfy him, and at length asked Phra Chamnan if he had no others to show him—especially larger stones.

By this time the latter was beginning to chafe at all his best stones being criticized in this offhand manner, and besides, he had no larger ones in stock; so he suddenly thought of the glass stopper that Kroh Dee had left with him. At first he felt too ashamed to bring it out, for it went hard against the grain of the first gem dealer in Bangkok to say that a piece of cut crystal was a real diamond, but still he had no finer stones to show the Lao, and he had begun to realize that the latter had no real knowledge of precious stones. So he brought out the stopper in a nonchalant kind of way and, with every appearance of excuse, said, "As you don't seem to like any of my stones, perhaps you would care to look at this. It is not mine, and I don't guarantee it, but it has been deposited with me for sale, and possibly it may suit you."

No sooner had the Lao picked up the stopper and examined it, than he turned to Phra Chamnan and said, "This is just what I am looking for. The size is exactly right and the water is good. If the price is reasonable, my business ends here. How much do you want for it?"

Then the gem merchant thought rapidly to himself, "It's true that Kroh Dee only wants ten *chang* for it, but if I ask only ten *chang* for a fine diamond of this size, the Lao may have his suspicions. I'd better not do that. Twenty *chang* would be nearer the mark, if the stone were a genuine one, and that would give me a profit of ten *chang* for myself. Anyhow, the man's a fool, and will probably pay what I ask."

So, after a moment's reflection, he turned to the Lao and said briefly, "The owner is demanding twenty *chang*," to which the Lao replied that the price was a very reasonable one, and that he would conclude the deal there and then. "Unfortunately," he continued, "I have not brought so much money with me. I have only five *chang* upon me at this moment. But I'll tell you what I'll do. I'll deposit these five *chang* with you now, and I'll bring the remainder within seven days. Then you can hand over the jewel. But before I go, if you have no objection, I would like to put the matter on a business footing, and sign a short agreement to this effect. If I do not return and pay the balance in seven days, then you may confiscate this five *chang* which I deposit now; but if I do bring the remaining fifteen *chang*, and for any reason at all you cannot hand me the jewel, then you must not only return me my deposit, but pay me a fine of five *chang* as well. You may not attach much importance to it, but I am not buying this gem for myself, and the contract will be a guarantee of good faith on both sides."

Phra Chamnan was inwardly highly amused and said, "You need not be afraid of me; I shall not sell the jewel to anybody else."

"I daresay not," said the Lao, "but all the same, I have to

cover myself, and unless you strongly object, I would like to make this contract now."

So the agreement was made, duly signed and witnessed, and the Lao took his leave of Phra Chamnan.

Two days after this incident Kroh Dee was passing Phra Chamnan's shop, and happening to find him at home, strolled in and said, "By the way, you remember that jewel I left with you some months ago to sell? Well, if you have not sold it already, I think I will take it back. I don't know where he comes from, but I hear there is a Lao in the town who is looking for fine diamonds, and it is quite possible that he might buy it from me. Have you been able to do anything with it?"

Now this simple request of Kroh Dee's placed Phra Chamnan on the horns of a great dilemma.

If he told the truth and said that he had already sold it to the Lao, Kroh Dee would quickly find out that the latter was paying twenty *chang* for it, and would claim its full value, especially as he himself has said that the gem was worth nothing. If he refused to pay, Kroh Dee might ruin his reputation. On the other hand, if he gave it back to Kroh Dee, he would have to forfeit five *chang* to the Lao, and that was out of the question. A moment's thought told him that there was only one way out of the difficulty. So, turning to Kroh Dee, he said, "Oh, you're asking about that stone of yours. Well, I have been examining it again, and I have now changed my mind. It's quite a good one, and if you like, I will buy it from you."

"But you said before that it was only worth a *fuang*," exclaimed Kroh Dee.

"Yes, I know I did, but I have changed my mind."

"Well, how much will you give me for it?" said Kroh Dee.

"Oh, I'll give you the price you were asking."

"All right, but don't you go about saying afterwards that I swindled you into buying a worthless stone for ten *chang*."

"No," said Phra Chamnan, "I'm quite satisfied about it now," and therewith he counted out ten *chang* to Kroh Dee, who put the money in his pocket and departed.

Phra Chamnan thought, of course, that he was making an excellent bargain, and waited impatiently for the seven days to expire. But the seven days went by, and eight, and nine, and ten, and still no Lao appeared. Then his heart began to sink within him, for, though he had the five *chang* which the Lao had left as a guarantee and had now forfeited, his gorge rose at the thought of the ten *chang* he had given to Kroh Dee for a worthless piece of glass. There was a clear loss of five *chang*.

Still the days went by without any sign of the Lao, and at last Phra Chamnan realized that he had been the victim of a clever trick at the hands of Kroh Dee, and that he, the gem dealer with the highest reputation in Bangkok, had been made to pay ten *chang* to an ignorant rascal for a bottle stopper which he had himself stated to be worth a *fuang*. And yet no action could he take without exposing himself to the ridicule of the whole town.

So there he sits in gloomy silence, still waiting for the Lao to return.

The River God's Wife
China

Long ago, in the days of Duke Wen of Wei, Ximen Bao was made commander of Ye. When he arrived at his post he assembled the local elders and asked them the cause of the people's suffering. The elders replied, "We suffer because the River God's marriages have brought poverty upon us."

Ximen Bao asked how this came to be. They replied, "Every year the high officials tax the people, and when they have collected several hundred thousand coppers they use two or three hundred thousand to pay for a wife for the River God, and divide the rest among themselves, saving a little for the shamaness who helps with the ceremonies.

"The shamaness surveys the local families, and when she finds one with a beautiful daughter, she says, 'This one shall be the River God's Wife.' Then she takes her away, bathes her, dresses her in silken robes, and causes her to fast. The people build a fasting pavilion beside the river, surrounded by silk curtains, and seclude the girl in it. They prepare meat, wine, and rice to eat, and after ten days they adorn the girl, spread out a mat, ask her to sit upon it, and send it down the river. At first it floats, but after a few dozen *li* it sinks.

"All the families with daughters are afraid that the shamaness will marry them to the River God, so they have fled far away. That's why our city has fewer and fewer people and is becoming poorer and poorer. This has been going on for a long time. The people have a saying, 'When the River God has no bride, floodwaters ravage far and wide.'"

Ximen Bao said, "The next time the River God takes a wife, and the officials and shamaness send her off, please let me know, so that I might see her off too." They replied, "Yes, Your Honor."

When the time came, Ximen Bao went down to the river, where the officials and elders were all assembled. Including the common people, there were two or three thousand observers all told. The shamaness was an old woman, more than seventy years old, and ten of her novices, all dressed in silk, stood there behind her.

Ximen Bao said, "Summon the River God's Wife, so that I may see how beautiful she is!"

They brought the girl out of the pavilion and led her to him. Bao looked at her, then turned and said to the high officials, the shamaness, and the elders, "This girl won't do. Might I trouble you, Shamaness, to inform the River God that we will have to look for a better bride, and that we will deliver her in a few days." Then he ordered his attendants to grab the shamaness and throw her into the river.

After a while he said, "What is taking the shamaness so long? Let's send a novice to hurry her up!" and they threw one of the novices into the river.

A little while later he said, "What is taking the novice so long? Let's send another to hurry her up!" and they threw another novice into the river. Altogether they threw in three of the novices.

Then Ximen Bao said, "The shamaness and her novices are all mere women, and they don't know how to get things done. Would you three officials mind going in to take care of this matter?" and they threw the three officials into the river.

Ximen Bao stood looking at the river for some time, while the elders and other observers all waited in fear.

Then Ximen Bao turned around and said, "Neither the shamaness nor the officials have come back. What shall we do?" He wanted to send the local elders in after them, but they all knelt down and kowtowed, knocking their heads against the ground so hard that blood flowed, and their faces turned pale as ash.

Ximen Bao said, "All right, let's wait a while."

After a while he said, "You may arise. It seems that the River God is detaining his guests, so we might as well go home."

From then on the people of Ye never again dared speak of the River God taking a wife.

"Of Course!"
China

Once upon a time there was a rich man whose nickname was Pepper-peel. He was a fierce-looking, cruel-hearted fellow who was exceptionally hard on his farmhands and tenant peasants.

Pepper-peel employed a farmhand from another province called Zhao Da. Zhao had worked for Pepper-peel six or seven years when one day he fell seriously ill. Pepper-peel weighed it up in his mind: From now on, Zhao would not only be useless for farm work, he would also be an extra mouth to feed. Without the slightest compunction, he drove him out of his house.

Zhao had toiled all these years for Pepper-peel. Although he had sweated like an ox, he had received nothing to eat but slops fit for a pig. He was left at the end without a penny to show for it. He struggled home as best he could, and when he got there, told his neighbors the whole story. They all felt that he had been wronged and vowed to avenge him. One of them suggested that they pool some money, use some of it to cure Zhao and take the rest into town to buy a fine parrot with a red beak and green feathers. They should train the parrot to say one thing and one thing only, "Of course!" He promised that by this means they could teach Pepper-peel a lesson. Everyone clapped and cheered.

A year passed. One day Zhao put on some smart clothes and, carrying the parrot, went to the rich man's house. He explained that he had come after all this time to pay his respects to his former master. Pepper-peel was startled to see him looking so prosperous. Hastily, he inquired, "Where have you been all this time? You seem to be flourishing.

What's that you've got there? It looks like a . . ." Zhao cut him short, "Oh, I manage to get by, thanks entirely to this."

Pepper-peel kept pressing him for more information. Zhao hemmed and hawed for a while before finally embarking on his story. He had been recuperating at home, he said, when one night a god appeared before him in a dream and told him where to find a remarkable parrot that knew all the places where gold and silver lay buried. He went to find the parrot and bought it for two strings of coppers, and from then on money began to come his way. The bird was a treasure that he took with him wherever he went.

Pepper-peel didn't believe his story and asked him to put the bird to the test. Zhao agreed to this. Carrying the parrot, he took Pepper-peel to a place where there was a well. "Pretty Polly," said Zhao, "is there silver buried here?" The parrot replied, "Of course!"

Zhao dug at once and unearthed a small pot of glittering silver.

They walked on and came to a place where there was a slight hollow in the ground. Zhao asked again, "Pretty Polly, is there gold buried here?" The parrot replied, "Of course!"

Zhao dug again and unearthed a small package of gold. By this time Pepper-peel's mouth was drooling. His only thought was how to buy this parrot.

The following day he gave a great banquet at his home and invited all the gentry and wealthy folk in the town. Thinking that Zhao would be too abashed to refuse in the presence of all these distinguished guests, he planned to conclude the purchase right in the middle of the banquet. The local gentry and wealthy folk were eager to see the curious bird and descended on his mansion like a swarm of bees, offering their smarmiest congratulations. After draining three cups of wine, Pepper-peel said to Zhao, "You must sell me your parrot. Simply name your price."

Zhao hesitated a while before replying, "You were my master for six or seven years. How could I possibly refuse in front of all these people? But this creature is a treasure. I must call on the guests to suggest a reasonable figure for the sale." "Don't worry," the guests reassured him. "We'll see to it that both sides get a fair deal."

Pepper-peel was beside himself with joy. His wife murmured in his ear, "Such a marvel is worth everything we have." Her advice sounded reasonable enough to Pepper-peel and he acted accordingly. In the presence of an intermediary and a witness, he made out the deed of sale and signed it. It stipulated that his property would all pass into Zhao's hands in exchange for the parrot. The guests crowded round to offer their congratulations once again.

Pepper-peel was overjoyed at having acquired the parrot. Enthusiastically, he picked it up and set off, followed by his hired thugs and a band of relatives and friends whom he had invited to come and watch him prospect for gold and silver.

They arrived at the bank of a pond and Pepper-peel asked, "Pretty Polly, is there silver buried here?" "Of course!" replied the parrot. They dug but found nothing. They walked on till they came to a mountain. Pepper-peel asked, "Pretty Polly, is there gold buried here?" The parrot replied, "Of course!" They dug but again found nothing. Since nobody had taken the trouble to bury anything there beforehand, it was hardly surprising. Pepper-peel realized that he had been cheated, and exclaimed, "Pretty Polly! You've deceived me!" "Of course!" replied the parrot. "Pretty Polly! You've taken me for a ride!" "Of course!" Pepper-peel's face went blue with rage and his eyes bulged out of his head. Cursing and swearing, he threw the parrot onto the ground, "You'll be the death of me, you wretched bird!" With a flap of its wings, the parrot flew up into the air and perched on a twig and cried, "Of course!"

King Bato and Asin
Philippines

King Bato Bukidnon had many servants. One of them, Asin, used to indulge in vain boasts about himself. Asin told the other servants one day, "I am the wisest among you all, as well as among all the courtiers and nobles in the palace. I challenge anyone to beat me at wisdom and sagacity."

This boast reached the ears of King Bato. He was somewhat irritated, and felt like putting Asin to a test.

Called to the court, Asin bowed low before the monarch of Bukidnon. He knew why he had been summoned, but he wasn't the least nervous.

King Bato addressed him: "We are told that you are the wisest man in this palace. We wish to see how you can prove it, and if you cannot, severe punishment awaits you."

"I am ready, Sire," said Asin nonchalantly.

"Go, catch the waves of the sea in a net," said the king, declaring the test.

"That's very easy, Your Majesty," rejoined Asin. "All I need, Sire, is a rope made of sand. If Your Majesty takes the trouble to provide me this rope, I shall catch the waves as desired."

King Bato was flabbergasted. He did not know what to say. He retired to ponder over a more difficult problem for Asin.

On the following day, Asin was again called to the court. The greetings over, King Bato handed him a small duck and said, "Take this and prepare fifty kinds of dishes out of it."

Asin was not be be beaten in this test either. Thinking on his feet, he rejoined, "I will surely do Your Majesty's bidding. But first I need a stove, a pan, and a knife made from this needle," and he handed a needle to the king.

223

Outwitted a second time, in the presence of the entire court, King Bato was really very angry with Asin. He shouted at him, "Get out of our palace! If anyone sees you anywhere in the palace or lurking in the garden, we will have you sent to jail for life."

"I understand, Sire," said Asin, making a quick obeisance, and he left the court and the palace.

Undeterred by King Bato's command, Asin was loitering around the palace on the following morning. King Bato was furious to see Asin riding on a sledge drawn by a small pony.

"Did we not order you not to walk on the ground around the palace?" shouted the king in righteous indignation. "What brings you here? You want life imprisonment, surely. No, we will have your head off for disobedience."

This time also Asin kept his composure. "Sire, Your Majesty can see," he replied deferentially, "that I am standing on my own earth, not your ground." Pointing to the earth on his sledge, he added for good measure, "This earth has come from my own land, Sire."

Conceding that Asin had again won, King Bato remarked, "Yes, you win this time too. I have, however, a conundrum for you."

Handing Asin a fairly big squash and a narrow-necked jar, the king added, "Put this squash into this jar. But you must ensure that the jar is not broken or the squash mashed."

Handling the two articles, Asin found that the squash was much too big to go into the very narrow neck of the jar. It was indeed a hard riddle, almost insoluble, but Asin would not readily admit to defeat. He took leave of the king and went home with the jar and the squash.

This was the first time that Asin had come home with an unsolved problem. More often than not, he would resolve issues on the spot and come home only for rest and recuperation after a hard working day at the palace.

Pondering over the problem for a long time, Asin sauntered to his garden. Squash, string beans, and other vegetables and plants grew there in abundance. Glancing at the squash plants, he noticed a small squash fruit. It was small enough to enter the neck of the jar given by the King.

Asin had an idea, perhaps the best that he had for a long time. He pushed the squash inside the jar without removing the fruit from the plant, and let it grow there inside.

Several weeks passed. The squash grew bigger inside the jar, pressing the sides as it were. Asin went to the king's court and presented the jar. King Bato was delighted to see the squash inside and the jar intact. Neither the jar nor the squash was damaged in any way.

This time King Bato said, "Asin you are a very clever man. We appoint you the head of the palace attendants."

Asin also received presents from the King. Thenceforth, King Bato used to consult Asin whenever he had a difficult problem to solve. Asin led a happy life as the trusted courtier of King Bato.

Ooka the Wise
Japan

Now it so happened in the days of old Yedo, as Tokyo was once called, that the storytellers told marvelous tales of the wit and wisdom of His Honorable Honor, Ooka Tadasuke, Echizen-no-Kami.

This famous judge never refused to hear a complaint, even if it seemed strange or unreasonable. People sometimes came to his court with the most unusual cases, but Ooka always agreed to listen. And the strangest case of all was the famous Case of the Stolen Smell.

It all began when a poor student rented a room over a tempura shop—a shop where fried food could be bought. The student was a most likable young man, but the shopkeeper was a miser who suspected everyone of trying to get the better of him. One day he heard the student talking with one of his friends.

"It is sad to be so poor that one can only afford to eat plain rice," the friend complained.

"Oh," said the student, "I have found a very satisfactory answer to the problem. I eat my rice each day while the shopkeeper downstairs fries his fish. The smell comes up, and my humble rice seems to have much more flavor. It is really the smell, you know, that makes things taste so good."

The shopkeeper was furious. To think that someone was enjoying the smell of his fish for nothing! "Thief!" he shouted. "I demand that you pay me for the smells you have stolen."

"A smell is a smell," the young man replied. "Anyone can smell what he wants to. I will pay you nothing!"

Scarlet with rage, the shopkeeper rushed to Ooka's court and charged the student with theft. Of course, everyone laughed at him, for how could anyone steal a smell? Ooka would surely send the man about his business. But to everyone's astonishment, the judge agreed to hear the case.

"Every man is entitled to his hour in court," he explained. "If this man feels strongly enough about his smells to make a complaint, it is only right that I, as city magistrate, should hear the case." He frowned at the amused spectators.

Gravely Ooka sat on the dais and heard the evidence. Then he delivered his verdict.

"The student is obviously guilty," he said severely. "Taking another person's property is theft, and I cannot see that a smell is different from any other property."

The shopkeeper was delighted, but the student was horrified. He was very poor, and he owed the shopkeeper for three months' smelling. He would surely be thrown into prison.

"How much money have you?" Ooka asked him.

"Only five *mon*, Honorable Honor," the boy replied. "I need that to pay my rent or I will be thrown out into the street."

"Let me see the money," said the judge.

The young man held out his hand. Ooka nodded and told him to drop the coins from one hand to the other.

The judge listened to the pleasant clink of the money and said to the shopkeeper, "You have now been paid. If you have any other complaints in the future, please bring them to the court. It is our wish that all injustices be punished and all virtue rewarded."

"But, most Honorable Honor," the shopkeeper protested, "I did not get the money! The thief dropped it from one hand to the other. See! I have nothing." He held up his empty hands to show the judge.

Ooka stared at him gravely. "It is the court's judgment that the punishment should fit the crime. I have decided that the price of the *smell* of food shall be the *sound* of money. Justice has prevailed as usual in my court."

◆

It was the day of the summer festival in Yedo, and Ooka had come down to the gate to see the parade go by his house. He especially wanted to see his grandson, Kazuo, who had been chosen to help pull one of the decorated wagons in the parade.

Ooka smiled to see all the happy faces around him. This

was truly a day for rejoicing, a day when everyone forgot his worries and joined in the celebrations. As the wagon which Kazuo and the other boys were pulling went by, Ooka glowed with pride. Only a sharp reminder to himself that it was undignified for a judge to show his feelings in public prevented him from waving and calling to his grandson.

Suddenly Ooka became aware that there was one sad face among all the happy people in the street. Not far away stood a woman with tears in her eyes. Ooka beckoned to her.

The woman came up to him and bowed respectfully. "Are you in trouble?" the judge asked her kindly.

"Please don't ask me, Lord Ooka," she replied. "It concerns my husband's family. And you know, it is not permitted for a wife to complain in these matters."

"That is true," Ooka said. "And it is a very wise law. However, if you were permitted to talk and if I were prepared to listen, then what would you complain about, may I ask?"

"About how badly his uncle, Tarobei, treats my son, Zensuke."

"I know Tarobei," Ooka said. "He is a fine man in many ways, but I hear he has the most terrible temper in all the city of Yedo."

"That is the cause of my son's trouble," the mother replied tearfully. "Two days ago, he began his apprenticeship in his uncle's shop."

"That is very good," Ooka remarked. "He will learn how to run a business."

"But, Lord Ooka, twice already the terrible-tempered Tarobei has become enraged with my son and thrown things at him. Once it was a serving spoon. Another time it was a cooking pot. I know the poor child is clumsy, but after all, he is only eleven."

"I see," Ooka said thoughtfully. "Naturally it would be most improper for your husband to complain to his elder brother about this."

He sat for a moment in silence and then said, "I will speak to him."

"Tarobei?" asked the woman eagerly.

"Certainly not," replied Ooka. "I shall speak to Zensuke."

"But, Lord Ooka, it is not the child's fault. He is new at his work. It is natural for him to make a few mistakes. If Tarobei would not frighten him so, he would not make so many."

"Nevertheless, I will speak to Zensuke," Ooka said. "I cannot speak to Tarobei, because you have not made a complaint against him. Have you forgotten? It is against the law."

Looking even more unhappy than before, Zensuke's mother made her way home, wondering if all the stories she had heard about Ooka's kindness to the poor could possibly be true.

The next day, Ooka paid a visit to Tarobei's shop. No sooner had he entered the street than he heard the tradesman's angry voice scolding the unfortunate apprentice.

Ooka hurried down the street and crossed toward the shop. As he did so, Zensuke came running out and, in his haste to escape the merchant's wrath, bumped into the judge. Both fell to the ground. This was fortunate, for it kept them from being hit by an iron rice pot Tarobei hurled after the fleeing boy, shouting, "Take that, you clumsy nincompoop!"

When the merchant saw how narrowly he had missed hitting the famous judge, he fell to his knees and touched the ground with his head, loudly begging Ooka's pardon.

Calmly Ooka got to his feet and silenced the apologetic merchant. "I wish to see this boy's apprentice agreement," he demanded.

The merchant hurried to obey. After glancing through the document, Ooka handed it back to Tarobei.

Ooka looked sternly at Zensuke and said, "According to

your apprentice papers, you are to be fed, clothed, and given a home or any presents your uncle wishes to give."

Zensuke nodded and looked at the ground.

"In return for this generous treatment, you are to serve your master faithfully for ten years."

"Yes! Yes!" Tarobei cried. Zensuke nodded again.

"Very well," Ooka continued. "I order you to work very hard to please your uncle."

Tarobei rubbed his hands in delight at the judge's words, while Zensuke, in a low voice, promised to do better.

Ooka smiled at him kindly. "I am sure you will," he said. "Now take your new iron rice pot and put it away for safe-keeping."

"My . . . my pot?" Zensuke said, puzzled.

"Of course!" Ooka replied. "The agreement says your master may give you presents if he wishes, and I clearly heard Tarobei say, 'Take that!' as he threw the pot. So it must be yours. Add to it the serving spoon and the cooking pot and anything else he has thrown at you. They, too, are yours."

"My lord!" Tarobei protested. "I didn't mean—"

"To throw the gifts at the child?" Ooka interrupted. "Of course you didn't. And you are to be congratulated on your surprising generosity to your nephew. If you continue to be so generous, Zensuke may own the shop someday."

Smiling at the flustered merchant, Ooka went back home, well pleased with himself.

From that day, Tarobei never again threw anything at his nephew. Zensuke, no longer afraid, made fewer mistakes. He became a fine worker, and soon everyone was happy in the shop of Tarobei.

◆

The typhoon came from the sea and slashed its way across the land. The wise bamboo bent with the wind and laughed at the storm. But stronger trees, fences and houses—not so sly as the bamboo—tried to stand up to the wind and were destroyed.

One of the houses destroyed was a home for orphans in the little town of Meguro near Yedo. To rebuild it, Ooka placed a special house tax on all the homes in the village. All owners were happy to pay except a crafty tea merchant named Tosuke.

"Why should a man who has no children have to pay a tax to build a new home for orphans?" he asked his wife. "Why, that silly judge has set the tax at one gold *ryo* for every door in the house. That would cost me six *ryo*. I will not pay it!"

"But, husband, Ooka will put you in prison if you refuse to pay," his wife said anxiously.

"I did not say I would refuse. I said I was not going to pay it," Tosuke replied. "You have a very clever husband. I intend to outsmart Ooka."

Tosuke joined the line of taxpayers before Ooka. When his turn came, Tosuke protested that a man without children should not have to pay the tax.

"It is necessary to build a home for these poor children," the old judge said. "It was set at one *ryo* for each door, because a poor man's house has only one. Richer houses have more. Kindly make your payment, and do it quickly before I become angry."

"I still say it is wrong," Tosuke said ungraciously, handing Ooka a single *ryo*.

"You have six doors! Where are the other five *ryo*?" Ooka asked.

Tosuke looked around to see if the other taxpayers were admiring his cleverness as he said, "Lord Ooka, before coming here I sealed up all but one door. Now my house has only one."

The great judge looked at him sourly. There was no law

which prevented a man from sealing up extra entrances, but Ooka knew he could not allow the sly tea merchant to out-smart him. Others would try the same trick. Slowly Ooka's ears turned red, a sure sign that he was embarrassed.

He said to Tosuke, "You are a rich man. It would not hurt you to pay this tax. Or even—"

Ooka paused and looked thoughtful. "Or even," he continued, "to care for all these twelve children yourself."

"My lord, I earned all I have by being frugal with my money. I see no reason to throw away a single *ryo.*"

Thoughtfully Ooka pulled at his beard and looked at the children gathered in the back of the courtroom. They were all shapes and sizes. They wore patched kimonos. They looked very sad.

"Look at those children," Ooka said to Tosuke. "Can you look into their faces and still say you should not help them?"

"I do!" Tosuke said firmly. "Why should I help someone outside my family? It is an injustice for me to pay even this one *ryo!*"

"An injustice? Oh, I cannot have an injustice blamed on my court!" Ooka said. "Perhaps I can think of some way so you will not have to pay any tax at all."

"Lord Ooka, that would be wonderful! You are truly the wise and just judge people have called you. I never realized it before."

"I hope you continue to think so," Ooka said with a slight smile. "Here is your gold coin back. You need pay no tax. Do you accept my decision?"

"I do!" Tosuke cried, touching the ground with his head to show his respect for so great a judge.

Before he could rise, Ooka, smiling blandly, called for a carpenter to go nail up the last door in Tosuke's house.

The startled tea merchant sat up. "What is this?" he asked.

"Since you are paying no tax, and the tax is for each door, you will not be permitted to have a door," Ooka explained.

"But how will I get in?"

"That is not my concern," the great judge said. "You didn't want to pay. And I found a way to keep you from having to do so. You should be pleased."

"But I live in my teashop. I can't get in to sell anything. I can't get in to eat and sleep. All my money is hidden inside."

"You should know that once I make a judgment I never change it. No one has any use for a judge who keeps changing his mind. You are dismissed."

Tosuke tried to persuade his neighbors to take him in. Angry at his greed, they refused. That night he and his wife slept in the street, huddled together to keep warm when the rain fell.

The next day, Tosuke, wet and miserable, came to Ooka's house.

"Lord Ooka," he cried. "You must help me."

"No tax, no door!" Ooka replied. "I never change my mind."

"Lord Ooka, I will be delighted to pay the whole six *ryo*."

"Impossible!" Ooka said. "I ruled you would not have to pay any tax. I cannot change that decision."

"But, great judge, you are famous for helping the poor. Now I am the poorest man in Japan. Please help me."

"Well, if you put it that way, perhaps I can do something. If you took these twelve children into your home, it would legally become an orphanage. Orphanages are not taxed, so you would have to pay nothing. I would not have to reverse a decision, the children would have a home, and all the people of Meguro would get back the taxes they paid. Everybody would be happy. Now that is the way justice should be."

"Take in twelve children? Lord Ooka, that is impossible! Do you know how much rice so many children would eat? And the amount of tea they would drink! And the—"

"I know how big your house is and how rich you are. This will not bankrupt you," Ooka said severely.

"Well, perhaps not, but it will still cost too much."

"You are wasting my time," Ooka said angrily. "Either take the children or be content with my decision."

Since he had no choice, Tosuke took the children. At first his life was miserable. He was disturbed by their noise and furious at their appetites.

But as time went on, he grew to like and finally to love them. And then it happened that Tosuke's taxless house was the happiest in all Japan.

Wise Magistrates
China

Once a pedlar of oil-cakes was on his way home after sell-ing a basket full of cakes. Feeling the need to ease the call of nature, he set down his basket on a rock and walked some distance from the road to relieve himself. When he returned, he found that all the money he had earned that day had disappeared from the place he kept it in the bottom of the basket. In great distress he rushed to the district magistrate to report the theft.

The magistrate ordered two of his servants to bring the rock to the courthouse for questioning. But though he interrogated it for half a day, the rock did not say a single word. The magistrate then ordered his servants to beat the rock, but they only succeeded in breaking the canes they used in the beating.

A crowd of onlookers laughed at the magistrate, making him so angry that he fined them each one copper coin. He made them file out of the courthouse one by one, dropping their coins into a wooden tub filled with water as they left. Suddenly he called out to one of the men, "Halt! You are the thief!" But the man would not admit his guilt.

The magistrate then gave the following explanation: "The pedlar was selling oil-cakes, and he kept all the money he earned in the bottom of his basket, where it became covered with oil. When the others threw their coins into the water nothing happened, but when you threw yours in a film of oil rose to the surface. That is how I know you are the thief." The man was forced to admit his guilt.

◆

*One day a firewood carrier laid down his bundle of fire-*wood and sat down under a tree by the side of the road to rest. Then along came a salt carrier who also eased the bundle of salt off his shoulders and sat under the same tree to rest. After a while, when they were ready to resume their journey, the two of them began to argue over a sheepskin, each claiming that the sheepskin belonged to him. Angry words turned into blows, and soon their clothes were torn and their faces bleeding. Neither would give in, so they took their case to the district magistrate for his decision.

The magistrate asked, "Why were you fighting?" The firewood carrier said, "The sheepskin is mine. I use it every day to protect my back when I am carrying wood. But he is trying to steal it from me." Then the salt carrier said, "The sheepskin is mine. I use it every day to protect my back when I am carrying salt. But he is trying to steal it from me."

The magistrate had his servant bring a mat to the courtroom, put the sheepskin on the mat, and beat it with bamboo poles. Salt crystals fell out from the sheepskin onto the mat, and the wood carrier had to confess that the sheepskin belonged to the other man.

◆

Once a man heard a thief in his house late at night, but by the time the man got up to confront him, the thief had escaped with the man's valuables.

The man took his case to the district magistrate, who rounded up the known thieves of the district and questioned them all, but none would confess. Then the magistrate said, "I have a temple bell which can discern thieves from honest men. If an honest man touches it, it will not make a sound, but if a thief touches it, it will ring out. Now I want each of you to place your hands on the bell. In this way I can find out who is the thief."

In the dark of night the magistrate secretly had his servants smear lampblack on the bell. Then he called the suspects before him and told each of them to touch the bell. When he examined their hands all were smeared with black save one man whose hands were clean. So the magistrate said, "You are the thief," and the man had to confess.

Poisonous Persimmons
Korea

A Buddhist priest once kept a big store of dried persimmons in a cupboard in his room. He planned to eat them all himself, and so he told his young disciple, "These are deadly poison. If you eat even the smallest part of one you will die within the hour. See that you leave them well alone."

But one day the young disciple went and ate all the persimmons in the cupboard. Then he broke the holder of his master's inkstone, which was his most highly prized possession, after which he went and lay on his bed and covered himself with blankets.

A little later the priest returned. When he saw his disciple he cried, "Whatever is the matter with you?" His disciple answered, "Through my miserable clumsiness I dropped the holder of your inkstone and broke it. I realized that that was an unpardonable crime. The only thing left for me to do was to put an end to my life, and so I went to your cupboard and ate all the poison you keep there. Now I lie here waiting to breathe my last."

The priest was so tickled by his disciple's ingenuity that he could not help laughing and said no more about the matter.

Shade Selling
Korea

It was a blistering hot day. A young man, feeling like he was broiling, looked across the field where he was working at a large *zelkova* tree in the distance. Smiling broadly, he started walking toward the tree which stood a few steps from the gate of a large house.

The young man was surprised to find a very well-dressed old man asleep on a rush mat under the tree. Not wanting to disturb him, the young man sat down very quietly to rest in the shade with his back against the tree and was soon dozing.

"You rascal! What are you doing sitting in someone else's shade?" screamed the old man.

The young man awoke with a start. "Excuse me. What did you say, sir?"

"I said what are you doing sitting in someone else's shade?" roared the old man.

The young man looked puzzled. "Someone else's shade? What do you mean 'someone else's shade?'"

"This is my shade!" screamed the old man. "Get out!"

"But this tree belongs to all the villagers," said the young man.

The old man snorted. "My grandfather's grandfather planted this tree. That makes it mine. Now get away from here!"

"I see," said the young man, nodding and smiling. "In that case," he said in a serious tone of voice, "would you be interested in selling me its shade?"

"Why sure," chuckled the old man. "I am the owner of the shade. Give me five *nyang* and it is yours."

The young man gave the old man five coins and, smiling broadly, lay down in the shade.

"Who would have thought there would be someone foolish enough to buy the shade of a tree," the old man chuckled to himself as he moved his rush mat to the shade of another tree.

As the sun moved across the sky, the shadow of the tree grew longer and extended into the old man's yard. After a while, the young man stood up and followed the tree's shadow into the yard and sat down.

"What do you mean coming into another man's yard!" roared the old man. "Get out of here you rascal!"

"Why? What's wrong, sir? All I'm doing is sitting in the shade you sold me," said the young man.

"Get out, you young impudent fool!" roared the old man.

"I think you are the one who should get out. You sold me the shade of that tree so I am entitled to go where its shade extends."

The old man was flabbergasted. He scowled and, muttering under his breath, stomped into his house.

Presently the young man followed the shadow of the tree to the old man's porch and lay down. Before long he stood up, opened the door and walked into the old man's living room.

"Get out! Get out of my house!" screamed the old man. But the young man just smiled and sat down.

When the shadow disappeared, the young man left the house and went home.

The next day and the next, day after day, the young man followed the shade of the tree into the old man's house.

Then one day the old man spoke to the young man in a subdued voice. "Please return the shade of the tree to me. I'll give you back your five *nyang*."

"I wouldn't think of returning this nice shade," replied the young man. "Now get out of it."

The old man could not go anywhere in the village without people pointing and laughing at him. The villagers called him "Greedy Old Shade Seller." "Do you have any shade for us?" they would jeer.

Finally, the old man and his family could not stand it any longer. They left the village in the middle of the night and were never heard of again.

The young man thus found himself the owner of the big house and he let everyone rest under the big *zelkova* tree beside his gate.

Ah Jin's Unlucky Words
China

The Wang family gave birth to a baby boy, and, as was the custom, they invited all their friends and relatives to a banquet when the baby was one month old.

Ah Jin was among those who received an invitation, but his neighbors counseled him not to go, because he had a habit of accidentally blurting out unlucky words like *die* and *death* on auspicious occasions, destroying the lucky atmosphere which the others were so carefully creating.

"If I promise not to say a word from beginning to end, do you think I could go?" he asked. His neighbors knew that his intentions were good, and agreed to take him along.

All during the banquet he kept his promise; he did not utter one word from the time the first toasts were drunk to the time the last sweet soup was served.

When the banquet was over and the guests were departing, Ah Jin stood at the doorway and took his leave saying, "All through the banquet I did not say a word, so if your son should happen to die, you can't blame me!"

The Magic Herb
China

Once there was a rich old man called Master Qian who owned many fields and houses. He rented out his land at exorbitant rates, and paid his hired hands the lowest possible wages. Though he was wealthy, he was very stingy, and he always looked for ways to deduct a few coppers from the pitiful wages he reluctantly gave his workers.

When the day came round to pay his laborers, he called them to him one by one. "Ah Fu!" he said, "I am going to take twenty coppers from your wages, because your dog has been running through my garden, trampling my flowers." Ah Fu seethed with anger, but there was nothing he could say.

"Ah Tu! Your hen has been pecking grain from my threshing floor. Thirty coppers less for you!"

After several months of such treatment, Ah Fu and Ah Tu decided to find a way to get back at Master Qian. At last they hit upon a plan.

One day when Master Qian had gone out, Ah Fu and Ah Tu stood under a tree, waiting for his return. When they saw him draw near they began whispering to each other, all the time pointing to a bird's nest in the tree. The inquisitive Master Qian asked them what they were looking at so intently, but Ah Fu and Ah Tu just appeared flustered and nervous, and replied, "N . . . n . . . nothing!"

This only increased Master Qian's curiosity and suspicion. He followed the two men and hid outside their window to eavesdrop on their conversation.

When Ah Fu heard Master Qian approach, he said to Ah Tu, "Let's try to get Master Qian to sell us that tree, and then the magic herb woven into the bird's nest will be ours." "Yes," said Ah Tu, "How lucky that we found the herb that makes its bearer invisible. With this magic herb in our possession we will no longer have to labor for Master Qian, but can make our fortune in the world."

Upon hearing these words, Master Qian said to himself, "So that's what they saw in the tree! The magic herb that makes one invisible! I must have it for myself!"

That night when everyone was asleep, Master Qian

propped a ladder against the tree, climbed up, and pulled
down the bird's nest. But he did not know which of the many
kinds of leaves and grasses woven in the nest was the magic
herb, so he woke up his wife and, holding one of the leaves in
his hand said to her, "Can you see me?"

"Of course I can see you!" she replied.

Picking up a strand of grass he said, "Can you see me
now?"

"Yes, I can still see you," she said, already somewhat im-
patient.

Master Qian would not give up, but tried again and
again with each different strand of leaf and grass from the
nest. At a certain point his wife could bear it no longer. She
was tired, and she did not understand this strange joke her
husband was playing on her. All she wanted was to go back
to sleep. So when he held up one particularly odd-shaped
leaf and asked his question again, she replied, "Now I can't
see you."

"Aha! I have found it!" he shouted, hardly able to contain his joy. He tossed and turned all night, unable to sleep
as he thought of ways to use his new possession.

The next morning he rose early and went into the city to
test the magic of his herb. As he went out the gate he saw
some herdsboys playing a game with marbles. Master Qian
grabbed a few of the rounded stones as he passed by. The
boys were about to cry out, but when they saw it was the
landlord who took their stones they held their tongues and
suffered in silence.

When Master Qian saw that the boys did not pursue
him, he smiled to himself, believing that his herb was at
work.

Inside the city, food vendors lined the streets, hawking all
kinds of tasty snacks. The fragrant smell of hot sesame
cakes reminded Master Qian that he had not yet eaten
breakfast, so he snatched a couple of piping hot sesame

cakes and began to eat them. The vendor was about to cry out, but when he looked up and saw it was his landlord he was afraid Master Qian would raise his rent, so he held his tongue and suffered in silence.

Master Qian was feeling bolder and bolder. "This herb is truly magic!" he said with great satisfaction.

After eating the sesame cakes he began to feel thirsty, and seeing a fruit vendor strolling by, with baskets of oranges on either end of a carrying pole, he boldly took an orange from one of the baskets as the vendor walked by. The vendor was about to cry, "Help! Thief!" but when he saw that Master Qian was dressed in satin robes he thought he might be an official from the courthouse, and it would not be a good idea to raise his ire, so he held his tongue and suffered in silence.

Now that Master Qian was sure the herb was magic, he said to himself, "What I have taken so far is small stuff. I wonder what I can take that will help me get rich? Aha! I have it! I will get the official seal from the courthouse, which is used to approve all sales of property. With this seal I can buy all the land in the county, for whatever price I like, and no one can say anything about it!"

He rushed to the courthouse and burst through the gate. The guards were used to seeing him there on business and let him pass without question. As it happened, the judge was at his dais, and the official seal was on the table in front of him. Master Qian walked boldly up to the table, grabbed the seal, and turned to walk away.

When the judge saw this he sat in stony silence for a moment, then rose and shouted, "Halt! How dare you try to steal the official seal, and in broad daylight too, when all can see! Guards, take him away and give him fifty strokes with the bamboo rod!"

"Have pity, Your Honor!" said Master Qian, amazed that his magic herb should have lost its power just at this moment. But the guards took him away and gave him fifty strokes with the bamboo rod, and it was too late for Master Qian to regret his folly.

The Foolish Son-in-law
China

Once there was a foolish young man who had the good fortune to marry a kind and sensible woman. His wife knew that he often did foolish things, so she took care to help him and instruct him whenever she could.

On the second day of the New Year the couple planned to visit his wife's parents, as was the custom. The wife gave her husband a basket of noodles, a live duck, and a bolt of cloth to take as presents. As her husband went out the door she said to him, "You go ahead, and I will follow close behind. Be careful of the presents—don't lose them or get them dirty. And another thing: You are not very good at making polite conversation, so just listen to what people along the road are saying, and use those phrases at my parents' house."

The foolish young man listened to what she said and set off happily for his parents-in-law's house, taking with him the duck, the noodles, and the bolt of cloth. Along the way he passed by a pond, and the duck began to quack. "He must be thirsty," thought the young man who, though foolish, was goodhearted. "I'll just let him have a drink from the pond." So he set the duck down and let him drink, but the duck swam away, and no amount of calling would bring him back.

"Well, I have lost the duck," he said to himself, "but perhaps I can catch a fish to take instead." Then he made a net out of the noodles, and tried to catch a big fish from the pond. But no sooner had he put the net into the pond than the noodles began to soften and dissolve, and the fish broke right through, so he had neither noodles, net, nor fish.

All he had left was the bolt of cloth. As he continued walking he passed by a bamboo grove, and he heard the sad sound of the bamboo sighing in the wind. "I wonder why the bamboo trees are sighing," he thought. "Perhaps they are cold, standing there in the wind with no clothes to keep them warm." So he took out his bolt of cloth and wrapped it around the bamboo, and continued his journey empty-handed.

Along the way he saw a pile of dung covered with flies. Another man walked by, startling the flies, which buzzed away. The man said, "Blue-green horseflies eating dung! See me coming and off you run!" The foolish young man had never heard this saying before, and committed it to memory, as his wife had suggested. A little farther down the road he saw a man mending a fence. When he asked him why he didn't tear the fence down and build a new one the man replied, "New poles, old poles, get by with what you've got." Though the foolish young man did not quite understand this saying, he committed it to memory too. A little later he came to a place where two streams, a muddy one and a clear one, ran together, and he heard a man say, "Two currents run together, but of a different color." The foolish young man thought this saying most profound, and memorized it also.

When he arrived at his parents-in-law's house he saw that his wife was already there. She had worried after he left, and brought another set of presents herself to her parents, and as he had dawdled along the way, she had arrived before him. When he explained to her what happened to the duck, the noodles, and the bolt of cloth, she sighed and said, "Never mind. I brought some presents myself. But now you must eat and drink with the menfolk, and I have thought of a plan so you won't make a fool of yourself. I will tie one end of a string to your leg, and I will stand behind the door holding the other end. When I give one tug on the string you should eat a mouthful of food, and when I give two tugs you should take a sip of wine. Don't forget!"

The foolish son-in-law happily agreed and sat down with the other men to eat. But who would have thought that a rooster would walk in at that very moment and begin pecking at the string. Peck, peck, peck! The foolish son-in-law thought that it was his wife tugging on the string, and he began to eat and drink, eat and drink, faster and faster as the rooster kept pecking. The other men at the table burst out laughing. Some spilled their wine, some dropped their chopsticks, some fell off their chairs and rolled on the floor.

Finally the rooster succeeded in breaking the string, and, feeling no more tugs, the foolish son-in-law stopped eating. When he saw the other men rolling on the floor he said, "Blue-green horseflies eating dung! See me coming and off you run!" The men were startled at his words, which seemed to be an odd sort of curse. After a moment the servants brought clean chopsticks and cups. The foolish son-in-law saw that they had given everyone else ivory chopsticks, but had given him bamboo, and this reminded him of the mended fence, so he said, "New poles, old poles, get by with what you've got." The men blushed a deep red, thinking that he had understood their insult, and they quickly replace his bamboo chopsticks with ivory ones.

When they were pouring wine, one relative who looked down on the foolish son-in-law poured inferior wine in his cup. The foolish son-in-law did not know that the wine was inferior, but he could see that the color was different from the others', so he said, "Two currents run together, but of a different color." The relative immediately blushed for shame, and exchanged the inferior wine for good.

After this, the relatives began to think that the son-in-law was not so foolish after all, that he had only been pretending to be foolish in order to expose their own petty trickery. As the rooster had broken the string, and the foolish son-in-law could no longer feel any signals to eat or drink, he just sat there silently as the others finished their meal, and this caused them to feel even more ashamed.

And so the foolish son-in-law and his wife enjoyed their visit, and returned home happily the next day.

FOREIGN LANGUAGES PRESS

"Ma Liang and His Magic Brush," from *The Frog Rider: Folk Tales from China, First Series,* Beijing, Foreign Languages Press, 1980. Used by permission of the publisher.

SUZANNE CROWDER HAN

"The Dog and the Cat," "The Tokkaebi's Club," and "Shade Selling," from *Korean Folk & Fairy Tales,* © 1991, by Suzanne Crowder Han. Hollym, Elizabeth, N.J., 1991. Reprinted by permission of the author.

HOLLYM CORPORATION

"The Sun and the Moon," "The Locust, the Ant, and the Kingfisher," "The Centipede Girl," "The Legend of the Virgin Arang," "The Magic Cap," "The Old Tiger and the Hare," and "Poisonous Persimmons," from *Folk Tales from Korea,* ed. by Zong In-sob. Hollym International Corp., Elizabeth N.J., 1982. Reprinted by permission of the president of Hollym Corporation, Shin-won Chu.

REGINALD LE MAY

"The Glass Stopper" and "The Story of Nai Prasop," from *Siamese Tales Old and New,* translated by Reginald le May. Noel Douglas, London, 1930.

NEW WORLD PRESS

"Of Course!" translated by John Minford, from *Favourite Folktales of China,* Beijing, New World Press, 1983. Reprinted by permission of Li Shujuan, Rights and Contracts Director, New World Press.

OXFORD UNIVERSITY PRESS

"The Mouse Lord Chooses a Bridegroom" and "Momotaro, the Peach Boy," © Oxford University Press 1969. Reprinted from *The Magic Mill-*

stones and Other Japanese Folk Stories by Barbara Hope Steinberg (1969) by permission of Oxford University Press.

SCOTT MEREDITH LITERARY AGENCY FOR I. G. EDMONDS

"Ooka and the Stolen Smell," "Ooka and the Terrible-tempered Tradesman," and "Ooka and the Tosuke's Tax," from *Ooka the Wise: Tales of Old Japan*, by I.G. Edmonds, Bobbs-Merrill Co., Inc., 1961. Reprinted by permission of the author and the author's agents, Scott Meredith Literary Agency, LP, 845 Third Avenue, New York, New York 10022.

STERLING PUBLISHERS

"The Turtle and the Monkey," "Rajah Soliman's Daughter," and "King Bato and Asin," from *Folk Tales of the Philippines*, by M. Mariano, New Delhi, Sterling Publishers, 1982. Reprinted by permission of the Managing Director of Sterling Publishers, S.K. Ghai.

YOSHIMATSU SUZUKI

"The Sea Palace" and "Kaguya Himé," from *Japanese Legends and Folktales*, Tokyo, Sakurai Shoten, 1949.

CHARLES E. TUTTLE CO., INC.

"How the Tiger Got His Stripes," "The Mosquito," and "The Story of Tam and Cam." From *Vietnamese Legends*, adapted by George F. Schultz, Tokyo, Tuttle, 1965. Used by permission of the publisher.

UNIVERSITY OF CHICAGO PRESS

"The *Oni*'s Laughter," "Little One Inch," "The Crane Wife," "The Tongue-cut Sparrow," and "The Salt-Grinding Millstones," from *Folktales of Japan*, ed. by Keigo Seki, Chicago, University of Chicago Press, 1963. Used by permission of the University of Chicago Press.

WEATHERHILL

"The Supernatural Crossbow," "The Dream at Nam Kha," and "The Da-Trang Crabs," from *The Land of Seagull and Fox: Folk Tales of Vietnam*, ed. by Ruth Q. Sun. Rutland, VT: Tuttle, 1967. Used by permission of Weatherhill.